Frederic George Kitton

The Novels of Charles Dickens

A bibliography and sketch

Frederic George Kitton

The Novels of Charles Dickens
A bibliography and sketch

ISBN/EAN: 9783337028923

Printed in Europe, USA, Canada, Australia, Japan

Cover: Foto ©Raphael Reischuk / pixelio.de

More available books at **www.hansebooks.com**

THE NOVELS

OF

CHARLES DICKENS

A BIBLIOGRAPHY AND SKETCH

BY

FREDERIC G. KITTON

AUTHOR OF "DICKENSIANA," "CHARLES DICKENS BY PEN AND PENCIL," ETC.

LONDON

ELLIOT STOCK, 62, PATERNOSTER ROW

1897

PREFACE.

T is said that the stories of England's favourite novelist owe their popularity mainly to the fact that they appeal to the "masses" rather than to the "classes." This is probably true, for it was that vast majority of the "world's workers" to which Dickens extended his sympathy, being prompt to recognise in its midst noble instances of worth, manliness, and humanity which are there so often manifested. He loved his fellow-men, and by means of his wonderful romances did more to increase the social happiness and morality of the humbler members of the community than any writer of his time. "If ever man left the world

better than he found it," remarks Mr. James Payn, "it was Charles Dickens." That being so, Thackeray's asseveration was a just one, when, on referring to his brother-novelist, he spoke of him in a most reverent tone as "the Jesus Christ of Literature."

It is difficult to realise to what extent Literature would have suffered if the novels of Dickens had never seen the light, or "to conceive" [quoting Mr. Andrew Lang] "how poor the world of fancy would be, 'how dispeopled of her dreams,' if, in some ruin of the social system, the books of Dickens were lost!" The principal characters he created are ever remembered as distinct types, while his phraseology constitutes part of our language; he is so eminently in request for fancies and general illustrations, that (as Professor Masson has pointed out) even those who are for writing him down find them indispensable, and are ever ready to avail themselves of some Dickensian touch of humour or pathos, the expression of which flashes on the mind the thought which is intended to be conveyed.

Dr. Oliver Wendell Holmes used to say of Dickens: "He is the greatest of all of them. Such fertility, such Shakspearean breadth—there is enough of him; you feel as you do when you see the ocean." The late Mr. William Morris considered that the author of "Pickwick" is immeasurably ahead of the novelists of our generation, an opinion fully endorsed by the Poet Laureate, when, in 1870, *he wrote: "He is unquestionably as far above all other English novelists, as Shakespeare is above all other English dramatists." In Mr. Swinburne's "Studies in Prose and Poetry" we read: "Dickens, I am happy to think, can hardly have had a more cordial and appreciative admirer than Mr. Jowett"* [*the late Professor Jowett, of University renown*]. *"Tennyson, Browning, and Carlyle were all still among us when I once happened to ask him whom he thought the first of living English writers. He hesitated for a minute or so, and then replied, 'If Dickens were alive, I shouldn't hesitate.'" Seldom has a more sympathetic tribute been penned in honour of any author than that by Mr. Swinburne himself, whose lines addressed to Charles Dickens will be found in his volume of verse entitled "Tristram of Lyonesse and Other Poems":—*

"Chief in thy generation born of men;
Whom English praise acclaimed as English born,
With eyes that matched the world-wide eyes of morn
For gleam of tears or laughter, tenderest then
When thoughts of children warmed their light, or when
Reverence of age with love and labour worn,
Or god-like pity fired with god-like scorn,
Shot through them flame that winged thy swift live pen."

NOTE.—For much information contained in the following pages I am principally indebted to Mr. Forster's "Life of Charles Dickens" and "The Letters of Charles Dickens," while many interesting details have been obtained from other biographical and bibliographical sources. My cordial acknowledgments are here tendered to Mr. W. R. Hughes, F.L.S., Treasurer of Birmingham, Mr. J. F. Dexter, and other ardent Dickensians, for valuable assistance rendered during the preparation of this volume.

FREDERIC G. KITTON.

ST. ALBANS.
March, 1897.

CONTENTS.

THE

NOVELS OF CHARLES DICKENS.

"THE PICKWICK PAPERS."

CHARLES DICKENS commenced his literary career in 1833, when in his twenty-second year. Before his appearance in the realm of Literature, he had officiated as a reporter for the *True Sun*, the *Mirror of Parliament* (conducted by his uncle, Mr. Barrow), and the *Morning Chronicle*, and it is recorded that, although so very juvenile, he occupied the very highest rank among the eighty or ninety reporters for the Press then in Parliament. But the youthful stenographer yearned to take a more important position than that offered by journalism; he aspired to publicity and fame as a writer of fiction, for which profession he was remarkably well endowed by Nature, possessing as he did, even during the days of his boyhood, a wonderful imagination and power of description.

Charles Dickens's first attempt in this direction appeared in the *Monthly Magazine* for December, 1833. The title of the little production was "A Dinner at Poplar Walk," and it was succeeded by other papers of a humorous and descriptive character. To the *Morning Chronicle*, the *Evening Chronicle*, *Bell's Life in London*, and "The Library of Fiction" the young writer contributed a series of clever articles and storyettes during 1835-36, all of which were subsequently published, with supplementary papers, as "Sketches by Boz." To Mr. James Grant, editor of the *Monthly Magazine* in 1836, Dickens stated (in reply to a request for a further supply of "Sketches") that he had just entered into an arrangement with Messrs. Chapman and Hall to write a monthly serial, which would occupy much spare time from his duties as a reporter. He did not then mention the name of the new venture, but it soon became known as "The Pickwick Papers." The first public intimation that the work was in course of preparation was made by means of the following advertisement in the *Times*, March 26th, 1836 :—

THE PICKWICK PAPERS.—On the 31st of March will be published, to be continued monthly, price One Shilling, the first number of the POSTHUMOUS PAPERS OF THE PICKWICK CLUB, containing a faithful record of the Perambulations, Perils, Travels, Adventures, and Sporting Transactions of the Corresponding Members. Edited by Boz. Each Monthly Part embellished with four Illustrations by Seymour. Chapman and Hall, 186, Strand; and of all Booksellers.

Mr. Charles Whitehead (then editor of "The Library of Fiction") was desired by Messrs. Chapman and Hall to associate himself with Robert Seymour in the production of a book which afterwards became famous as "The Pickwick Papers." Seymour was a popular artist of the day, whose humour found its most congenial themes in the mishaps attending the unskilful efforts of cockney sportsmen, and it appears very probable that a serial publication first issued by Messrs. Chapman and Hall in November, 1835, called the *Squib Annual of Poetry, Politics, and Personalities*, with sporting plates by Seymour, was the actual origin of "Pickwick." It is a curious thing, however, that in "Maxims and Hints for an

Angler" (1833), published before the *Squib Annual*, is revealed an elderly individual (also drawn by Seymour) marvellously like Mr. Pickwick in *physique* and benignity of expression; so that it seems as if the artist, whose first idea of the founder of the Club represented him as a long, thin man, only reverted to an early conception when he converted him into the rotund, jovial-looking gentleman whose personal appearance is so familiar to us. When the publishers offered Whitehead the commission to write to Seymour's designs, he declined on the ground that he was not equal to the task of producing the "copy" with sufficient regularity, and recommended the young author of the "Sketches by Boz." Messrs. Chapman and Hall, who had newly started in business, were therefore anxious to secure the services of Charles Dickens (then only two- or three-and-twenty years of age), and applied to him to write for them a monthly serial—the exact nature of the proposed work not being clearly defined—which was to serve as a vehicle for some plates by Seymour.

It was originally suggested that Messrs. Chapman and Hall's new serial should describe the proceedings of a "Nimrod Club," the misadventures of whose members by flood and field would afford the artist ample scope for displaying his peculiar talents. Dickens, however, being "no great sportsman, except in regard of all kinds of locomotion," preferred more liberty in the choice of scenes and characters than such an arrangement would allow, and considered "it would be infinitely better for the plates to arise naturally out of the text." The publishers agreeing to this modification, Dickens "thought of Mr. Pickwick," and invented Mr. Winkle for Seymour's special benefit; and it was from the proof-sheets of the first number that the artist drew the picture of the Club, including the portrait of Mr. Pickwick to which the novelist referred as having "made him a reality."

Mr. Mackenzie Bell considers it possible that the title of "The Pickwick Papers" may have been suggested to Dickens by a passage in the Preface to Whitehead's romance of "Jack Ketch," where a humorous allusion is made to the probability of the author producing "his more mature experience under the unambitious title of 'The Ketch Papers.'" It has also been insinuated (but not derogatively) that the first notion of "Pickwick" was derived by Dickens from Pierce Egan's "Life in London" and its sequel, where may be found certain characters somewhat similar to those in "Pickwick"—notably that of the "Fat Knight," the counterpart of Mr. Pickwick, who meets Corinthian Tom at the village of Pickwick, near Corsham, Wilts! In other details there is also a similarity; for instance, King's Bench Prison is introduced instead of the Fleet, and the archery-match instead of the shooting-party. There is no doubt that Dickens, like other great authors, borrowed many ideas from previous writers, *à propos* of which Mr. Forster points out that Smollett gave the hint of Sam Weller's transference of himself to the prison in order to serve Mr. Pickwick, while it is equally plain (as Dr. Bayne has indicated) that the incarceration of Jingle was suggested by that of Jenkinson in "The Vicar of Wakefield." Lord Jeffrey saw a resemblance between Mr. Pickwick and Don Quixote; indeed, "Pickwick" has been alluded to as a free translation of the famous Spanish romance into the manners of modern England, Mr. Pickwick being the hero and Sam his companion, Sancho.

"The Pickwick Papers" were issued in twenty monthly numbers, commencing April, 1836, and ending November, 1837, the last two Parts forming a double number. Each Part, the price of which was a shilling, appeared in a green wrapper bearing a design by Seymour, representing scenes of fishing and shooting, with trophies of sporting implements. The first number consisted of twenty-six pages of text and four etched illustrations. This arrangement did not entirely commend itself to those engaged in its production, but, before the question of alteration could be discussed, a tragic event happened on April 20th, 1836—the death of Seymour by his own hand. The second number contained an Address to the Public, in which the sad incident was announced, and an apology made for the appearance of three plates instead of four. "When we state that they". [viz., the illustrations] "comprise Mr. Seymour's last efforts, and that on one of them in particular (the embellishment to the Stroller's Tale) he was engaged up to a late hour of the night preceding his death, we feel confident that the excuse will be deemed a sufficient one." It was further affirmed that the publishers intended to present the ensuing numbers of "The Pickwick Papers" on an improved plan,—a promise duly fulfilled, for the quantity of letterpress was increased to thirty-two pages, and the number of plates diminished to two, in each succeeding monthly Part. Much difficulty was now experienced in finding another designer. Eventually Mr. R. W. Buss, "a gentleman already well known to the Public as a very Humorous and Talented Artist" (says the Address in the third number), was employed, but, being unaccustomed to the technicalities of etching, the two plates produced by him proved unsatisfactory, and were therefore cancelled after only a few copies of the Part containing them (No. 3) had been circulated. This failure on the part of Buss created a fresh vacancy for an illustrator, and it is interesting to learn that an application for the post was made by Thackeray, who submitted some specimens of his work to Dickens, which the latter, "strange to say, did not find suitable," as Thackeray himself remarked years afterwards. John Leech also aspired to the position, and with a like result. Another competitor was Hablôt K. Browne ("Phiz"), then a young artist, only known as having, at the age of seventeen, gained a medal for a capital etching of John Gilpin. Happily, he was elected, and first heard of his success from, and received the congratulations of, his generous and less fortunate rival, who felt no ill-will on account of his rejection, which he always humorously alluded to as "Mr. Pickwick's lucky escape." Thus commenced, in the fourth number of "Pickwick," Hablôt Browne's long association with the writings of Charles Dickens. As Seymour was the pictorial originator of Mr. Pickwick, so was "Phiz" the artistic creator of Sam Weller, the illustration in which that popular favourite first appears being his initial effort, although priority of publication was given to another design.

The expectations entertained of the possible success of "Pickwick" were modest in the extreme. Mr. Aked, the binder, has stated that he received the first order for binding Part I., and that it was for four hundred copies only (which contained the original etchings by Seymour), so that he was able to execute it himself in one evening after the work-people had left. The publishers sent out, "on sale or return," fifteen hundred copies of each of the first five numbers to all parts of the Provinces, the result being an average sale of only fifty copies of each number! So far, the venture was practically a failure, and it was seriously debated whether it should be discontinued or not. Fortunately, at this important juncture, Sam Weller was introduced to the public, and called forth such admiration by the freshness and originality of the conception, that the sale of the ensuing numbers suddenly increased,—so much so, that at the termination of the work the circulation had attained to forty thousand copies! The publishers were naturally delighted with this highly favourable state of affairs, and, when the twelfth number was reached, expressed their gratification by presenting the author with a cheque for £500.

"Pickwick" is by no means a consecutive or uninterrupted narrative, but rather (as it purported to be) an account of the adventures of Mr. Pickwick and his friends, interspersed with short tales which the author had already written, and which were probably intended as contributions to a new volume of "Sketches." The object of the work, at first, was simply to amuse, by placing before the reader "a constant succession of characters and incidents; to paint them in as vivid colours as he" [the author] "could command; and to render them, at the same time, life-like and amusing." The cumbrous machinery of the "Pickwick" Club was soon dispensed with, and the narrative allowed to run more smoothly in consequence.

Respecting Dickens's financial arrangements with his publishers, it has been affirmed that there was no agreement about "Pickwick" except a verbal one; but Mr. Augustin Daly, of New York, possesses a copy of a letter (dated February 12th, 1836) addressed to the novelist by Messrs. Chapman and Hall, where they mention the terms upon which they were prepared to publish the book—viz., that each number was to consist of a sheet and a-half, for which the author was to receive nine guineas a sheet, and that, if the work proved successful, he would be further remunerated.*

During publication Dickens received from Messrs. Chapman and Hall cheques amounting to £3,000, in addition to the stipulated payments, and it was stated by the novelist that, during three years

* Fifteen guineas per number was the amount as stated by Mr. Edward Chapman to Mr. Forster; but in a letter (dated 1835) to Miss Hogarth, soon afterwards to be his wife, Dickens mentions the sum as fourteen pounds,—and that "the emolument is too tempting to resist." He was paid for the first two numbers at once, as he required the money to marry with. Mr. J. F. Dexter informs me that a formal agreement was subsequently drawn up, which document he purchased of the late Mr. Fred. Chapman, at the sale of whose effects another copy was disposed of, probably a duplicate.

(1836-39), the publishers made a clear profit of £14,000 by the sale in numbers only. And this from a work which was once very nearly abandoned as hopeless!

Sam Weller, as we have seen, was the actual turning-point in Dickens's fortune, and the enthusiastic reception with which he was so deservedly welcomed doubtless determined the author to adopt Literature as a profession. His prospects having considerably improved, he married, and removed from chambers at 15, Furnival's Inn, Holborn (where the earlier portion of "Pickwick" was written), to more congenial quarters in Doughty Street, whence is dated the dedication of the book to his friend Serjeant Talfourd, M.P.

Before many numbers of "Pickwick" had been issued Dickens was prostrated with grief occasioned by the terribly sudden death, at the age of seventeen, of his sister-in-law, Mary Hogarth, who constituted his ideal of girlhood, and to whom he was tenderly attached. Owing to this mental shock the publication of "Pickwick" was interrupted for the space of two months,* the author being unable during that time to continue the work. In consequence of this, a variety of

* The fourteenth number is dated "May, 1837," and the fifteenth, "July, 1837."

rumours were circulated, which only tended to show the extraordinary interest felt by the public for the unknown author, whose name had not then been publicly announced. It was, indeed, "generally deemed impossible" [remarks a contemporary] "that such a work, so varied, so extensive, and yet so true in its observations, could be the production of any single individual; that it was the joint production of an association, the different members of which transmitted their various ideas and observations; that one of their number, whose province it was to reduce them to a connected form, was, and had for many years been, a prisoner in the King's Bench!" The same writer continues: "Of the many conjectures as to the non-appearance of No. 15 at the proper time, that which most nearly approached the truth was, that the author was a young gentleman of about eighteen years of age named Dickens, a Catholic, and bred to the Bar. To this it was added that his health was so much impaired by his literary exertions that there was not the slightest chance of his ever publishing another number." * Dickens, who had naturally been made aware of

* *Vide* MS. notes in a copy of "Pickwick," British Muscum.

such "idle speculations and absurdities," issued an Address in the fifteenth number, explaining the reason of the delay, and from that time matters went smoothly until the publication of the final instalment.

When "The Pickwick Papers" were published in volume form, the pseudonym of "Boz" was discarded, and the writer's actual name placed on the title-page; whereupon a certain ingenious critic attempted to prove that directly Dickens assumed his proper name there was a decline in the merit of his works!

Although at first "The Pickwick Papers" excited comparatively little attention, the work was very soon received with astonishing fervour on every side,—a fact rendered more remarkable when the juvenility of the author is remembered. The book was in everybody's hands, and formed the subject of conversation everywhere. As a proof of this extraordinary popularity, it is recorded that tradesmen on the look-out for novelties named their goods after the book about which every one was talking; and in the shop-windows were seen Pickwick chintzes, Weller corduroys, Pickwick cigars, Pickwick hats, Pickwick canes (with tassels), Pickwick coats (of peculiar cut and colour); Boz cabs rattled through the streets, Pickwick clubs (of a convivial character) were inaugurated, and the portraits in omnibuses of other public favourites were pasted over to make room for that of Charles Dickens. There were a "Pickwick Comic Almanac," a "Pickwick Treasury of Wit," a "Pickwickian Songster"; also a "Sam Weller's Pickwick Jest-Book" and "Sam Weller's Favourite Song-Book." The late Mr. Sala, in alluding to the early days of what people used to call "Bozomania," says that dogs and cats used to be named "Sam" and "Jingle," and "Mrs. Bardell" and "Job Trotter." Even to-day we have Pickwick and Boz pens, Pickwick biscuits, and Pickwick cigar-lights with a metal box to hold them, the latter representing that famous stone bearing the inscription, "Bilst um pshi s. m. ark." There also exists a fraternity called the Pickwick Bicycle Club, the oldest cycling club in existence, which was formed in June, 1870, at the time of the novelist's death, the members each choosing a *nom de guerre* from the pages of "Pickwick," the captain adopting that of the hero himself.

In 1849, a remarkable and absurd claim respecting "Pickwick" was made by the widow of Seymour, the artist, who endeavoured to prove (by means of a pamphlet, now very scarce) that to her husband belonged the credit of its conception, and that Dickens's assertions respecting his own share of the undertaking were altogether fallacious. Mrs. Seymour declared that the artist first conceived the idea of "The Pickwick Papers" in the summer of 1835, "and, but for a cold (which brought on a severe illness) which he caught on Lord Mayor's Day, on taking his children to view the procession from the Star Chamber, the book would have been written, as well as embellished, by himself; this cause alone prevented him from doing so, as the numerous periodicals he was constantly engaged upon had greatly accumulated during his illness."* Seymour's son published a letter in the *Athenæum*, March, 1866, where he repeated these statements, and Dickens immediately wrote a crushing reply (dated March 28th) in the same journal. The novelist emphatically

* "An account of the Origin of the 'Pickwick Papers.' By Mrs. Seymour, widow of the Distinguished Artist who Originated the Work. With Mr. Dickens's version, and her reply thereto, showing the fallacy of his statements; also letters of her husband's and other distinguished men. London: Printed for the Author, 2, Drayton Villas, Old Brompton." [1849.]

denied the gross imputation, averring that Seymour "never originated, suggested, or in any way had to do with, save as illustrator of what I devised, an incident, a character (except the sporting tastes of Mr. Winkle), a name, a phrase, or a word, to be found in 'The Pickwick Papers.'"

There are altogether three hundred and sixty characters in "Pickwick," and the prototypes of some of these have been readily identified. The hero himself, Mr. Samuel Pickwick,* was pourtrayed from John Foster, a friend of Mr. Chapman (the publisher); he is described as "a fat old beau who would wear, in spite of the ladies' protests, drab tights and black gaiters," and who lived at Richmond. The name "Pickwick" was taken from that of a Bath coachman, Moses Pickwick, which Dickens had seen painted on the door of a stage-coach. It has been suggested that Sam Weller's living original was Simon Spatterdash, a character in Beazeley's play of "The Boarding House," whose chief peculiarity lay in his quaint sayings and out-of-the-way comparisons, the part being taken by Samuel Vale, a popular low comedian of

* The daily papers of May 2nd, 1862, record the death of a Samuel Pickwick.

that day.* The name "Weller" may, of course, be a corruption of Vale, but it seems more probable that Dickens adopted the cognomen of the nurse of his childhood, whose maiden name was Weller. As a matter of fact, Weller is by no means an uncommon name, and it is interesting to learn in this connection that a younger brother of the novelist (Frederick) married the daughter of a Mr. Samuel Weller.

The legal gentlemen in "Pickwick" are nearly all portraits of people with whom Dickens came in contact during his clerkship days in Messrs. Ellis and Blackmore's office (1827-8). Mr. George Lear, a fellow-clerk with Dickens at this time, is convinced he stood for the portrait of the Articled Clerk, and that another colleague in the same office, named Potter, was not only the original of the Salaried Clerk described in the thirtieth chapter, but figures still more prominently as the redoubtable Alfred Jingle, his personal appearance being faithfully reproduced in the illustration representing Dr. Slammer's defiance of Jingle. The presentment of

* The late Dr. Donaldson discovered that the fashion of Sam's gnomic philosophy is at least as old as Theocritus, in proof of which he used to translate with great gusto a passage from *Idyll*, XV. 77. *Vide* Prof. Ward's "Dickens."

the doctor, by the way, is said to have been taken from Dr. Lamert, a regimental surgeon at Chatham, and an uncle of the novelist. Mr. Lear believes that Dickens himself was one of " the office lads, in their first surtouts," as mentioned in the thirtieth chapter. Mr. Blackmore inclined to the belief that Mr. Perker was intended as a delineation of his partner, Mr. Ellis, who certainly indulged in incessant snuff-taking. Serjeant Buzfuz is a fairly accurate likeness of Mr. Serjeant Bompas, an eminent counsel at that time, while the peculiarities of Mr. Justice Gazelee were suggested by those of Mr. Justice Stareleigh. As a proof of the continued vitality of " Pickwick," it is worthy of mention that on December 3rd, 1895, at the South-Western Police Court, Mr. Cluer adopted Dickens as an authority on evidence, quoting the famous ruling of Mr. Justice Stareleigh in the notorious breach-of-promise case, " Bardell *v.* Pickwick," that " what the soldier, or any other man, said is not evidence." Tony Weller's living original was recognised by Mrs. Lynn Linton in " Old Chumley," who drove the stage daily between Rochester and London. That designing widow, Mrs. Bardell, is reputed to have been drawn, " with a free and faithful touch," from a Mrs. Ann Ellis, who kept an eating-house near Doctors' Commons; while a certain Mr. Winters, who had a habit of ogling the ladies in Hyde Park and at fashionable watering-places, was acknowledged by his friends to be a *facsimile* of the too susceptible Mr. Tracy Tupman. The real name of the original of Joe, the Fat Boy, was James Budden, whose father kept the "Red Lion," at the corner of Military Road and High Street, Chatham. He was related to the Budden family in the "Boz" Sketch entitled "Mr. Minns and his Cousin."

Mr. J. Harold Bailey, M.B., has a word of praise for Dickens's representations of certain members of the medical profession, who were doubtless depicted from the life. "Ben Allen and Bob Sawyer," he says, "may be rightly termed the classical medical students of fiction. Even at the present time, many of the lay public form their idea of medical students from these classical types."*

It is amusing to read the early predictions as to the fate of "Pickwick" and its author. One discriminating critic, availing himself of Tom Paine's familiar prophecy, remarked that Boz had "risen

* *Medical Magazine*, June, 1894.

like a rocket and would come down like the stick,"—that is, if he continued to write too often and too fast; and when the ninth number appeared, a writer in the *Athenæum* decried the work as being made up of "two pounds of Smollett, three ounces of Sterne, a handful of Hook, a dash of a grammatical Pierce Egan,—incidents at pleasure, served with original sauce *piquante.*" In the Preface to a subsequent edition Dickens wrote: "My friends told me it was a low, cheap form of publication, by which I should ruin all my rising hopes: and how right my friends turned out to be, everybody now knows."

Remembering that Dickens received little or no assistance from the Press, the success of "The Pickwick Papers" was amazing. The book was devoured alike by judges on the bench (Lord Denman, to wit) and by boys in the street; both old and young revelled in its pages. Carlyle, whose adverse opinion of "Pickwick" was doubtless considerably modified in after-years, once related an anecdote of a solemn clergyman who, as he left the room of a sick person to whom he had been administering ghostly consolation, heard the invalid ejaculate, "Well, thank God, 'Pickwick' will be out in ten days, anyway!"

Sir Benjamin Brodie, at that time the head of the medical profession in England, read "Pickwick" in his carriage while travelling from patient to patient; and, greater tribute still, Lord Chief Justice Campbell once told Dickens that he would prefer the prestige of having written "Pickwick" to the honours which his professional exertions had obtained for him! Professor Ruskin (who loves Dickens "with every bit of my heart," and sympathises "in everything he thought or tried to do, except in his effort to make more money by readings, which killed him") declared that "Pickwick" always amuses him when he is well, "though I have known it by heart" [he adds], "pretty nearly all, since it came out." Dean Stanley invariably resorted to "Pickwick" when depressed in spirits, as its perusal inevitably cheered him. Miss Harriet Martineau considered that in humour Dickens would hardly surpass "Pickwick," "simply because 'Pickwick' is scarcely surpassable in humour"; and Miss Mitford, when advising a friend to read "The Pickwick Papers," spoke enthusiastically in praise of the work, describing it as being "so graphic, so individual, and so true that you could curtsey to all the people as you see them in the streets."

There are probably not more than a dozen copies of the first edition of "Pickwick" in existence. An examination of a number of impressions presumably of this edition results in the discovery of slight variations both in plates and text. These are especially noticeable in the illustrations, for, owing to the enormous demand, the plates were re-etched directly they showed signs of deterioration in the printing, and "Phiz," in reproducing his designs, sometimes altered them slightly. The earliest impressions of the work may be distinguished by the absence of engraved titles on the plates, and by their containing the *original* etchings by Seymour and Buss, not "Phiz's" *replicas* of them. In 1889, a unique copy of "Pickwick," in the monthly parts, was disposed of for £50, being probably the first issued from the press; it was the author's own copy, each number of which he presented (up to the date of her death) to Mary Hogarth, and afterwards, until completion, to her father, George Hogarth. A perfect original copy should include seven illustrations by Seymour, two by Buss, and thirty-four by "Phiz," all without titles; also the four Addresses issued in Parts 2, 3, 10, and 15 respectively. *Collation*—pp. xiv., two unnumbered pages, and pp. 609. The first Cheap Edition contains a frontispiece by C. R. Leslie, R.A., and a new Preface, dated "London, September, 1847," the latter being considerably amplified in the "Charles Dickens" Edition of twenty years later.

The original manuscript of "The Pickwick Papers" was never preserved intact. A fragment (comprising Chapters XXXV. and XXXVI.), with other Dickens MSS., was purchased at Sotheby's for £51 by Mr. C. B. Foote, of New York, and re-sold in 1895 in the United States for thrice that sum, with a portion of the "Nickleby" manuscript, and a copy of the following humorous lines in the autograph of the novelist, which were addressed to a member of the printing staff:—

"*Private and Confidential.*

"To Mr. Hicks.

"Oh, Mr. Hick
—s, I'm heartily sick
Of this sixteenth 'Pickwick,'
Which is just in the nick
For the publishing trick,
And will read nice and slick,
If you'll only be quick! .
I don't write on tick,
That's my comfort, avick!"

On June 14th, 1889, there was sold at

Sotheby's a modest-looking scrap-book which contained a very important collection of Dickens Ana, including an autograph letter from Dickens to Robert Seymour, a portrait of that artist, with several early impressions of his "Pickwick" plates, and, most attractive of all, six original drawings by him for "Pickwick." This interesting collection realised the enormous sum of £500, the purchaser being Mr. Augustin Daly. To Mr. William Wright, of Paris, belong the remaining "Pickwick" drawings by Seymour and "Phiz."

Mr. C. S. Calverley (author of "Poems and Translations" and "Fly Leaves"), when lecturer of Christ College, Cambridge, issued a paper on "Pickwick," after the model of the usual examination paper, containing questions relating to the most out-of-the-way details, thus forming a crucial test of scholarship. The prizes were copies of the first edition of "Pickwick," the fortunate competitors being Sir Walter Besant and Professor Skeat. Another, and less familiar, item was printed and published by J. Vincent, at Oxford, and by Whittaker & Co., London, in 1855, which took the form of a pamphlet entitled "The Student's Guide to the School of 'Litteræ Fictitiæ,' commonly called Novel-Literature." It contains five divisions, the last of which comprises a series of Examination Questions, together with a "Pickwick" Examination Paper, and other queries relating to the various writings of Dickens.

"OLIVER TWIST."

LONG before "Pickwick" was completed Dickens had commenced "Oliver Twist." It would seem as though the marvellous success of the former work compelled the youthful author to realise the magnitude of his powers, and thus induced him to essay a higher and graver style of art. On August 22nd, 1836, he entered into an agreement with Mr. Richard Bentley, the well-known publisher, to edit a monthly magazine, which was christened *Bentley's Miscellany.* It was also arranged that the novelist should at once furnish the new periodical with a serial tale, and that Mr. Bentley should purchase of him two or more stories for subsequent publication, one of these being "Barnaby Rudge." The first number of the *Miscellany* was issued in January, 1837, but the initial chapter of the editor's contribution, entitled "Oliver Twist, or, the Parish Boy's Progress," with illustrations by George

Cruikshank, did not appear until February. The story was continued during the three following months, and in the June number a Note was inserted, stating that the author was so prostrated with grief by "the sudden death of a very dear young relative to whom he was most affectionately attached"* that he was compelled to seek an interval of rest before he could again devote attention to the story. It was resumed, however, in July, and carried on from that date until its conclusion in March, 1839, when Dickens yielded the editorship of the *Miscellany* to his friend Harrison Ainsworth. That the youthful and indefatigable "Boz" was greatly worried by stress of work, during the first year of his connection with the magazine, is not surprising when we remember that he was simultaneously engaged upon several literary productions. Besides "Oliver Twist," he had in hand the latter half of "Pickwick," the early chapters of "Nicholas Nickleby," the editing of the "Memoirs of Joseph Grimaldi," and other writings of a less important character, the latter including further contributions to *Bentley's* which were afterwards published under the

* His sister-in-law, Mary Hogarth.

general title of "The Mudfog Papers." Under these circumstances Dickens experienced such mental tension that he felt as if (to use his own expression) he "had something hanging over him like a hideous nightmare." "I no sooner get myself up," he said, "high and dry to attack Oliver manfully, than up come the waves of each month's work, and drive me back again into a sea of manuscript." We cannot wonder, therefore, that he retired from the editorial chair at the first opportunity.

Concerning the preparation of "Oliver Twist," which was written at 48, Doughty Street, Mr. Henry Burnett (Dickens's brother-in-law) has placed on record the following interesting incident, which indicates how the novelist could concentrate his thoughts while a chatty conversation was proceeding :—

"One night in Doughty Street, Mrs. Charles Dickens, my wife and myself were sitting round the fire, cosily enjoying a chat, when Dickens, for some purpose, came suddenly from his study into the room. 'What, you here!' he exclaimed; 'I'll bring down my work.' It was his monthly portion of 'Oliver Twist' for *Bentley's*. In a few minutes he returned, manuscript in hand, and while he was pleasantly discoursing he employed himself in carrying to a corner of the room a little table, at which he seated himself and recommenced his writing. We, at his bidding, went on talking our 'little nothings,'—he, every now and then (the feather of his pen still moving rapidly from side to side), put in a cheerful interlude. It was interesting to watch, upon the sly, the mind and the muscles working (or, if you please, *playing*) in company, as new thoughts were being dropped upon the paper. And to note the working brow, the set of mouth, with the tongue tightly pressed against the closed lips, as was his habit."

Mr. Forster relates that as the story shaped itself it took an extraordinary hold upon its author, who could hardly leave it, working more frequently after dinner and until later hours than was his custom with any other of his novels. In May, 1838, Dickens wrote to his biographer with reference to it: "I worked pretty well last night, very well indeed; but although I did eleven close slips before half-past twelve I have four to write to complete the chapter; and, as I foolishly left them till this morning, have the steam to get up afresh." Again, a month later: "I got to the sixteenth slip last night, and shall try hard to get to the thirtieth before I go to bed." In the beginning of August he wrote: "Hard at work still. Nancy is no more. I showed what I have done to Kate" [his wife] "last night, who was in an unspeakable '*state*': from which and my own impression I augur well. When I have sent Sikes to the devil, I must have yours." "No, no," he remarked, in the following month; "don't, don't let us ride till to-morrow, not having yet disposed of the Jew, who is such an out and outer that I don't know what to make of him."

In a letter to his friend Serjeant Talfourd, July, 1838, Dickens said: "It is indispensably necessary that 'Oliver Twist' should be published in three volumes in September next. I have only just begun the last one, and, having the constant drawback of my monthly work, shall be sadly harassed to get it finished in time, especially as I have several very important scenes (important to the story, I mean) yet to write." It was in that very month named by him that the final chapter was penned. In the first week of September he invited Mr. Forster to lunch with him, "and sit here, and read, or work, or do something, while I write the LAST chapter of 'Oliver,' which will be arter a lamb chop." "How well I remember that evening!" says Mr. Forster, "and our talk of what should be the fate of Charley Bates, on behalf of whom (as indeed for the Dodger too) Talfourd had pleaded as earnestly in mitigation of judgment as ever at the bar for any client he had most respected." On November 9th, 1838 (that is, about four months before its completion in *Bentley's*), the entire story was published, at twenty-five shillings, in three volumes post octavo, with the twenty-four etchings by Cruikshank which accompanied it in its serial form. A remarkable fact has lately been divulged concerning this three-volume edition, viz., that only 528 copies were originally subscribed for by the trade, which copies were distributed among no less than thirty-five booksellers and librarians, and realised £463 16*s*. 9*d*.

The amount of remuneration received by Dickens for "Oliver Twist" is not recorded by Mr. Forster, but some interesting information respecting the book has recently come to light in a letter from the author to Mr. Bentley, dated July 14th, 1837:—

"First, that you should give me £600 for permission to publish 300 [*sic*] copies of my first novel, 'B. R.' ["Barnaby Rudge" *], this number to be divided into as many editions as you think well, and the whole of the manuscript to be

* "Barnaby Rudge" was not begun until more than two years later.

furnished by the 1st March, 1838, at the latest.

"Second, that for permission to publish the same number of copies of my second novel, 'O. T.' [" Oliver Twist "], you should give me £700, deducting from that amount all you may have been made to pay for the appearance of the different portions of it in the *Miscellany* up to the time of my finishing the whole manuscript, which I promise, at the very latest, shall be Midsummer next.

"I have considered the subject very carefully, and this is the fixed conclusion at which I have arrived. I am sure it is a fair and very reasonable one, but if you are resolved to think differently, of course you have the power to hold me to the old agreement. However, if you hold me to the strict letter of the agreement respecting the novels, I shall abide by the strict letter of my agreement respecting the *Miscellany*, and arrange my future plans with reference to it accordingly." *

From a statement published by Mr. Bentley, we learn that the novelist at first agreed to accept £500, the fee

* A *facsimile* of a shorthand copy of this letter, together with a transcript thereof, appeared in the *Strand Magazine*, January, 1896.

being afterwards increased to £750. Dickens referred to this payment as "a paltry, wretched, miserable sum," and, conceiving that the publishers were profiting very considerably by the publication of the story in book form, he determined to repurchase the copyright in order that he, as the author, might reap some of the pecuniary benefits accruing from the sale. Bentley magnanimously consented to the rupture of the agreement, released Dickens from his contract to write "Barnaby Rudge," and made over to him in June, 1840, the copyright of "Oliver Twist" and such printed stock (1,002 copies) as remained of the second edition, together with the Cruikshank illustrations, for the sum of £2,250.

"Oliver Twist" was the first of Dickens's romances that was subjected to the revision of his friend Mr. Forster, who read and suggested corrections to everything which the novelist afterwards wrote. As Dickens anticipated, the outcry raised by the book was great; it was objected to "on some very high moral grounds in some very high moral quarters," and was particularly aspersed by partisans of the Poor Laws and Workhouse system as a gross exaggeration and distortion of facts. In his Preface the novelist protested against such harsh and unjust conclusions, confessing that he had "yet to learn that a lesson of the purest good may not be drawn from the vilest evil," and averring that he "saw no reason why the very dregs of life, so long as their speech did not offend the ear, should not serve the purpose of a moral." Of those who admired the romance (and they were many) was his famous contemporary, Thackeray, who said: "The power of the writer is so amazing, that the reader at once becomes his captive, and must follow him whithersoever he leads. . . . The pathos of the workhouse scenes in 'Oliver Twist' is genuine and pure."* Anthony Trollope considered that, "Of all Dickens's novels, 'Oliver Twist' is perhaps artistically the best, as in it the author adheres most tenaciously to one story, and interests us most thoroughly by his plot."† Serjeant Talfourd, who said that it was the most delightful tale he had ever read, composed a laudatory sonnet, "To Charles Dickens, on his 'Oliver Twist,'" which is published in his "Tragedies," etc. (1844).‡ Mr. Wilkie

* *Fraser's Magazine*, February, 1840.

† *Nineteenth Century*, January, 1879.

‡ Serjeant Talfourd's copy of "Oliver Twist," presented by the author, was sold in 1889 for £39.

Collins, in his own marked copy of Forster's Life of Dickens, wrote that "the one defect in that wonderful book is the helplessly bad construction of the story"; and that "the character of Nancy is the finest thing he ever did. He never afterwards saw all sides of a woman's character—saw all round her. That the same man who could create 'Nancy' created the second Mrs. Dombey is the most incomprehensible anomaly that I know of in literature."

Cruikshank claimed the credit of having originated the idea of the book, as well as of its principal characters and incidents. Dr. Shelton Mackenzie, in describing an interview he had with the artist, states that Cruikshank declared that when Dickens once called upon him he was much struck with certain sketches which he found in the artist's studio, and obtained permission "to write up to as many of his designs as he thought would suit his purpose," the particular drawing which most attracted his attention being a representation of Fagin in the "condemned" cell, this tempting him to change the whole plot of his story. In a letter to the *Times*, as well as in a pamphlet subsequently written by him, entitled "Artist and Author—a Statement of Facts" (1872), Cruikshank repeated these details, and affirmed that in the presence of Dickens and Ainsworth he described and performed the character of one of the Jew receivers, this being (he alleged) the origin of Fagin. Mr. Forster, however, characterises this explanation as "a marvellous fable"; the artist may have possibly suggested details in the plot of "Oliver Twist," but that he overstated his case through the power of a vivid imagination is more than probable. The unfortunate controversy doubtless recalled to the artist's memory a little unpleasantness that arose concerning Dickens's rejection of an etching made for "Oliver Twist," called "The Fireside Scene," which the novelist thought so unsatisfactory that he insisted upon its being cancelled. Writing to Cruikshank on the subject, he said: "Without entering into the question of great haste or any other cause which may have led to its being what it is, I am quite sure there can be little difference of opinion between us with respect to the result. May I ask whether you will object to designing this plate afresh, and doing so at *once* in order that as few impressions as possible of the present one may go forth?" As a substitute for the "Fireside" plate, Cruikshank etched an entirely different picture, representing Oliver, with Rose Maylie, standing before his mother's tomb, which cannot be considered an improvement on its predecessor.

That "Oliver Twist" served its purpose no one will venture to dispute, for it was doubtless owing to the writer's vigorous denunciation of a pernicious system of conducting workhouses, and of "Bumbledom" in general, that salutary reforms have since been effected in the direction of decency, humanity, and common-sense. It has likewise led (indirectly, perhaps) to the formation of institutions for the benefit of waifs and strays like poor Oliver; as, for example, those homes for destitute children founded in our own day by such public benefactors as Dr. Barnardo, who, on the occasion of a presentation of which he was lately the recipient, remarked that he well remembered Oliver Twist. "I know him intimately," he said, "by many different names, and I also know Noah Claypole; and Fagin I meet in Houndsditch, Short's Gardens, and Fulwood's Rents. The Artful Dodger was an early capture in Fulwood's Rents. As for Mr. Bumble, he is not dead yet, though

I am thankful to say that in many instances the autocratic official has been dismissed from his 'porochial' duties. Whereas poor Oliver Twist was the rule when I caught my first street arab, he is now the exception in the slums. Oliver has come into his rights."

In this story the novelist wrote out of office a certain Mr. Laing (who figures as Mr. Fang), then a Clerkenwell magistrate, conspicuous for his coarseness and ill-temper. It is interesting to know that the name "Fagin" was taken from that of a youth engaged at the Blacking Warehouse on Hungerford Stairs, where Dickens in his boyhood found temporary occupation; this lad explained to the future novelist the trick of using the string and tying the knot.

The original issue of "Oliver Twist" contained no preface or dedication, and the collation is as follows: Vol. I. One unnumbered page (List of Plates), pp. 331, nine illustrations; Vol. II. pp. 307, seven illustrations; Vol. III. pp. 315, eight illustrations. The present price of the first issue with the cancelled plate is from £6 to £7; with the substituted plate, £4 to £5. An edition bearing the same date (1838), having on the title-page "Charles Dickens" instead of

"Boz," is not the genuine first issue, although it is often mistaken for it. A third edition (so called) was issued, with a Preface, by Messrs. Chapman and Hall, in 1841.* A new edition in ten monthly parts, demy octavo, each part in a green wrapper having thereon a pictorial design by Cruikshank, was commenced in January, 1846, the price being one shilling each number. It was subsequently published for the author in one volume—pp. xii., 311—at eleven shillings, by Messrs. Bradbury and Evans, and contained (as did the parts) all the Cruikshank plates, which, however, had suffered so much from previous wear-and-tear as to necessitate a general touching-up—indeed, some of them had additional backgrounds

* Mr. J. F. Dexter informs me that there were four issues of "Oliver Twist" before the third edition (so called) appeared, and he believes there may be one or two others. The following is a list of these early issues:—

1st. With cancelled plate, 1838. By "Boz."
2nd. With substituted plate, 1838.
By Charles Dickens.
3rd. " " "
(Second Edition on title), 1839.
By Charles Dickens.
4th. Same title as first issue, 1840.
5th. Third Edition on title, 1841.
By Charles Dickens.

added, and were otherwise tampered with by Findlay, much to the disgust of Cruikshank himself. The price, in numbers, is from £6 to £8, and in cloth, £3 to £4; a very choice copy, in parts as issued, was recently sold at Sotheby's for the handsome figure of £15. The late Mr. F. Burgess had previously paid £22 10*s.* for this very copy. The first Cheap Edition (with a new Preface) was brought out in 1850 by the same firm, as part of a new series; this also appeared in numbers, with green wrappers, and was afterwards sold in volume form at three shillings and sixpence, with a frontispiece only by Cruikshank.

The greater part of the MS. of "Oliver Twist" is in the Forster Collection at South Kensington. It is bound in two volumes, beginning with the twelfth chapter, and ending with the sixth chapter of the third book. The missing fragments of the MS. were lost or destroyed during the clearing out of the publisher's warehouse in the absence of Mr. George Bentley, and it is owing to an industrious search afterwards instigated by him through the papers which remained that the existing portions are preserved. A part of this MS. was purchased for £50 by Mr. Forster at Sotheby's on July 23rd, 1870, and on the same occasion the original Prospectus of *Bentley's Miscellany*, in Dickens's autograph, realised £10.

"NICHOLAS NICKLEBY."

ACCORDING to the terms of an agreement, dated November 18th, 1837, it was stipulated that Dickens should deliver to his publishers, on March 15th, 1838, the initial number of a new story, to be completed in twenty monthly parts. In April of the latter year the first instalment was launched from the press, its full title being "The Life and Adventures of Nicholas Nickleby, containing a Faithful Account of the Fortunes, Misfortunes, Uprisings, Downfallings, and Complete Career of the Nickleby Family." As in "Oliver Twist" the novelist had exposed the shortcomings of the Poor Law system, so, in the new venture, he determined to deliver a vigorous protest against the then prevailing method of conducting cheap boarding-schools, especially those in Yorkshire, which, for the most part, deserved the strongest denunciations. Of these seminaries Dickens had heard terrible accounts during his boyhood at Rochester, which made such a lasting impression upon his mind that he decided to learn as much as possible concerning the accuracy of the revelations which had so horrified him. He therefore, with this special object in view, paid a visit to the locality where schools of the worst repute were situated, setting out on his journey northwards at the end of January, 1838, and accompanied by Hablôt K. Browne (more familiarly known as "Phiz"), the versatile artist who succeeded Seymour as illustrator of "The Pickwick Papers." Forewarned that the Yorkshire schoolmasters might resent a visit from the author of "Oliver Twist," he consulted a solicitor-friend who had a Yorkshire connection, and between them they concocted "a pious fraud" in the form of letters of introduction, having reference to "a supposititious little boy who had been left with a widowed mother" anxious to place him at a school in the neighbourhood. The person to whom one of these was addressed was, as the novelist himself afterwards affirmed, the original of John Browdie in the story. On arriving at the "George" Inn, Greta Bridge, Dickens (when writing to his wife) described the principal incidents of this trying journey by coach during severe wintry weather, and thus concluded his letter: "Having finished our discoveries, we start for Barnard Castle, which is only four miles off. All the schools are round about that place, and a dozen old abbeys besides, which we shall visit by some means or other to-morrow. We shall reach York on Saturday, I hope (February 3rd), and, God willing, I trust I shall be at home on Wednesday morning." He found himself at Barnard Castle on February 1st, staying only two nights in the town, and was in London again five days later.

Dickens commenced the new story on the very day of his return home with his hastily-scribbled notes and memoranda. Although engaged upon "Oliver Twist" until its completion in September, he worked hard at "Nickleby," and his correspondence at this date shows that he never had a single number ready in advance—indeed, in some instances, it was uncertain whether he would come up to time. On February 7th, 1838 (which was his birthday anniversary), he wrote to Mr. Forster: "I *have* begun! I wrote four slips last night, so you see the beginning is made. And what is more, I can go on: so I hope the book is in training at last." A fortnight later he announced the completion of the first chapter, but in the second number a serious difficulty presented itself: "I could not write a line till three o'clock," he says, "and have yet five slips to finish, and don't know what to put in them, for I have reached the point I meant to leave off with." This obstacle was speedily overcome, however, and when he had the story well in hand he wrote: "I must be alone in my glory to-day, and see what I can do. I perpetrated a great amount of work yesterday, and have every day indeed since Monday, but I must buckle-to again and endeavour to get the steam up. If this were to go on long, I should 'bust' the boiler. I think Mrs. Nickleby's love-scene will come out rather unique." On September 9th, 1839, Mr. Forster received this note: "I am hard at it, but these windings-up wind slowly, and I shall think I have done great things if I have entirely finished by the 20th." On the 18th, he said: "I shall not entirely finish before Friday. . . . I have had pretty stiff work as you may suppose, and I have taken great pains. The discovery is made, Ralph is dead, the loves have come all right, Tim Linkinwater has proposed, and I have now only to break up Dotheboys and the book together." His labours were concluded on the 20th, at Broadstairs, and the fact is thus recorded under that date in his private Diary: "Finished Nickleby this day at two o'clock, and went over to Ramsgate with Fred and Kate, to send the last little chapter to Bradbury and Evans. Thank God that I have lived to get through it happily;" and in the next entry (September 21st) we read: "To town to-day (by steam from Ramsgate) to correct proofs. Dined with Forster, and went carefully through the whole No. with him. We did not finish till past midnight; slept at home. Wet through, weary, and happy to have finished."

The payment originally agreed upon (based on the financial results of the sale of "Pickwick") was to be made, in twenty sums of £150 each, on the fifteenth day of every month during the run of the story. For this remuneration the publishers acquired the copyright for five years, after which time it was to revert to the author, together with a share of the copyright of "Pickwick." That its success was complete and immediate is proved by the fact that the sale of Part 1 reached, on the first day, nearly fifty thousand. At the conclusion of the story, the novelist received from the publishers a handsome honorarium of £1,500 over and above the sum nominated in the bond. It was at this time that Dickens began to have his place as a writer conceded to him, and "ceased to be regarded as a mere phenomenon or marvel of fortune."

"Nicholas Nickleby" was published in the stipulated number of parts at one shilling each, with illustrations by "Phiz," the first number appearing in April, 1838, while the two final parts were issued simultaneously in October, 1839. The story was then published complete in one volume, demy octavo—pp. xvi., 624—with an Inscription to Macready, the actor. It contained thirty-nine illustrations by "Phiz" and a portrait of the author as frontispiece, beautifully engraved by Finden from the painting by D. Maclise, R.A.* The first Cheap Edition was issued in 1848, with a new Preface and a frontispiece representing the famous brimstone-and-treacle scene at Dotheboys Hall, from the picture by T. Webster, R.A. A French translation by P. Lovain, authorised for publication in Paris by Dickens in 1857, includes an Address by the novelist to the French public, which is also to be found in other

* This portrait now hangs in the National Gallery.

volumes of the French edition of the novelist's works.

A good copy of the original edition in parts is valued at about £4, while a bound copy realises from £2 to £3. The most amusing fragment of the few portions of the original MS. that have been preserved is that containing Fanny Squeers's letter to Ralph Nickleby (now in the possession of a New York collector), which Leigh Hunt considered as far surpassing the best things of the kind in Smollett. The manuscript of Chapters IX., XV., and XVII. of the story (all that is extant, I believe, and which includes the above-mentioned letter) was sold at Sotheby's in 1883.

The Rev. Sydney Smith once disparaged Dickens, but the witty Canon afterwards confessed himself vanquished. "'Nickleby' is *very good*," he wrote when the sixth number appeared. "I stood out against Mr. Dickens as long as I could, but he has conquered me." Thackeray, too, when lecturing in 1857 at St. Martin's Hall, took occasion to mention the fondness children always have for Dickens's works, and notably his own daughter's infatuation for "Nicholas Nickleby." As an instance of its great attraction for juveniles, it may be mentioned that when the story was approaching completion Dickens received, through the author of the "Ingoldsby Legends," a letter from a little boy (Master Hastings Hughes) with suggestions as to the fate of the various characters, to which the novelist replied in a very humorous fashion, addressing his young correspondent as "Respected Sir," and informing him how he intended to punish the bad characters and reward the good ones.

The intended conclusion of "Nicholas Nickleby" was anticipated by the drama tists, and Dickens, naturally annoyed by this proceeding, was compelled to alter the termination of his story. In the succeeding number he dropped down heavily on these dramatic pirates, by introducing his hero in conversation with a "literary gentleman" (intended as a portrait of W. T. Moncrieff), who, after expressing an opinion that it advances the fame of an author to have his work dramatised by him, is subjected by Nicholas to a wholesome tirade against the malpractices indulged in by members of his particular craft. A French playwright also adapted it for the Parisian stage, and its performance was witnessed by Thackeray, who wrote an amusing account thereof in *Fraser's Magazine*, March, 1842.

It has been estimated that "Nicholas Nickleby" contains one hundred and seventeen "speaking" characters, and that twenty-five more are named, making a total of one hundred and forty-two. As the *Saturday Review* remarked, "They were not studies of persons, but persons. They were alive; they were themselves." The original of Miss La Creevy, the good-natured little miniature-painter, was probably Miss Rose Emma Drummond, to whom, in 1835 (three years before "Nickleby" was begun), Dickens sat for his portrait on ivory; this presentment was executed as an "engagement" gift to his future wife, and is now in the possession of Mrs. Perugini. The name and personal peculiarities of Newman Noggs was derived from an impoverished gentleman, Newman Knott, whom Dickens frequently saw at the office of Messrs. Ellis and Blackmore, during his own clerkship days. Vincent Crummles, in the flesh, is said to have been the manager of a provincial theatrical company, who afterwards emigrated to America, and the late Mr. W. P. Davidge, an American actor of repute, stated that the portrait was drawn from an old Thespian named Davenport, whose daughter, Mrs. General Lander, was "the Infant Phenomenon."

The portrait of Mrs. Nickleby was based upon the personality of the novelist's mother,* while the individuality of Kate Nickleby was inspired by his sister Fanny, in whose husband, the late Mr. Henry Burnett (a professional vocalist), Dickens found the actual prototype of his hero. While the story was in progress Mr. Burnett often heard his name coupled with that of Nicholas Nickleby, concerning which he has placed on record some interesting reminiscences.†

Dickens's pictures of Squeers and Dotheboys Hall called forth an excitement scarcely less pronounced than that caused by his denunciation of the Poor Law system in "Oliver Twist." It is a curious fact that many Yorkshire schoolmasters were anxious to identify themselves with the original of Squeers—which

* In a letter to Mr. R. J. Lane, A.R.A., 1844, Dickens said, *à propos* of some people who looked upon certain of his characters as grotesque impossibilities: "Mrs. Nickleby herself, sitting bodily before me in a solid chair, once asked me whether I really believed there ever was such a woman!"

† Mr. Henry Burnett died at Titchfield, Hants, on February 7th, 1893, at the age of eighty-one, that day being, by a curious coincidence, the eighty-first anniversary of the birth of Charles Dickens.

pleased Dickens as much as it amused him. In his Preface he emphatically asserts that Squeers is "the representative of a class, and not of an individual"—that the notorious pedagogue and Dotheboys Hall are but "faint and feeble pictures of an existing reality." Notwithstanding these assurances, much has been published during recent years respecting this subject, some writers vigorously impeaching the accuracy of Dickens's statements. One of his critics harshly designated "Nickleby" as "a study in untruth," which "broke the hearts of two very decent people," while others affirmed (with apparent authority) that the real Dotheboys Hall was conducted on exemplary lines, that the scholars were perfectly healthy and well-looked-after; also, that the prototype of Squeers was really an amiable, good-natured man, and his daughter Fanny "one of the sweetest and kindest of women"! Sixteen years before "Nickleby" appeared, several actions were tried in London before Judge Park, in which the parents of children ill-used at a school kept by a Mr. Shaw were the complainants, the result being that the defendant Shaw was cast in heavy damages. Dickens has not only hinted, in the Preface, that he obtained many of his facts from the newspaper reports of such cases, but he entered in his private Diary (under date February 2nd, 1838) a memorandum which sufficiently proves that he had Shaw principally in his mind when describing Squeers and his establishment. He writes :—

> "Shaw, the schoolmaster we saw to-day, is the man in whose school several boys went blind some time since, from gross neglect. The case was tried, and the verdict went against him. It must have been between 1823 and 1826. Look this out in the newspapers."

It seems probable that the novelist's portrait too much resembled Shaw, who soon afterwards fell a victim to the obloquy which was due to that type of Yorkshire pedagogues generally. That such abominable schools once existed there can be no doubt, for it is stated that Richard Cobden spent five years of school-life at an actual Dotheboys Hall in Yorkshire, where he was "ill-fed, ill-taught, ill-used ; he never saw parent or friend ; and once in each quarter he was permitted to relieve his feelings by a letter home."

Perhaps no characters in fiction have excited more pleasurable feelings than the Cheeryble Brothers, who act as a distinct foil to the unpalatable Mr. Squeers and family. It is interesting to know that such genial personages as the Cheerybles had living prototypes, viz., the brothers Grant (Daniel and William), of Ramsbottom and Manchester. There were really four brothers, sons of a farmer, who, being ruined by a flood, afterwards became a herdsman; he and his boys were attracted by the blue-dye works contiguous to the Irwell, and, being naturally thrifty and energetic, soon saved sufficient money to invest in print goods, etc., with which they stocked a small shop in Bury, from which modest beginning they eventually became (by the special help of Sir Robert Peel) owners of extensive works at Ramsbottom, and by their industry, ability, and integrity were regarded as among the best men in their county. A memorial, called "Grants' Stone," marks the spot where the penniless youths rested (like Dick Whittington of old) while taking their first look at the town in which they were afterwards to make themselves a name and a fortune.

Dickens, who for many years possessed an engraved portrait of Daniel Grant, thus wrote to an American friend, Professor Felton, the letter being dated "Niagara Falls, 29th April, 1842": "One of the noble hearts who sat for the Cheeryble Brothers" [William Grant] "is dead. If I had been in England, I would certainly have gone into mourning for the loss of such a glorious life. His brother is not expected to survive him." [He died in 1855.] "I am told that it appears from a memorandum found among the papers of the deceased, that in his lifetime he gave away in charity £600,000, or three million dollars!" In his Preface to "Nicholas Nickleby" (1848 edition) the novelist declares that he never interchanged any communication with the Cheeryble Brothers in his life, so that his admirable presentments of them must have been produced by the aid of information derived from those well acquainted with the Grants.

"MASTER HUMPHREY'S CLOCK,"

INCLUDING "THE OLD CURIOSITY SHOP" AND "BARNABY RUDGE."

N the completion of "Nicholas Nickleby," Dickens decided upon a fresh form of publication. He considered it advisable to temporarily discontinue the plan of issuing his works in monthly parts, as the public (ever ready to welcome innovations) might tire of it; it also occurred to him that the establishment of a cheap weekly publication, not necessarily to be written entirely by himself, would somewhat relieve him of the labour entailed by the preparation of a long serial story, and prove at the same time very remunerative. In a letter to Mr. Forster (dated 1839), where the novelist entered into the details of his project, he proposed to start the new venture on the same lines as Addison's *Spectator*—that is, "with some pleasant fiction relative to the origin of the publication; to introduce a little club or knot of characters, and to carry their personal histories and proceedings through the work; to introduce fresh characters constantly; to re-introduce Mr. Pickwick and Sam Weller, the latter of whom might furnish an occasional communication with great effect; to write amusing essays on the various foibles of the day as they arise; to take advantage of all passing events, and to vary the form of the papers by throwing them into sketches, essays, tales, adventures, letters from imaginary correspondents, and so forth, so as to diversify the contents as much as possible. . . ."

Such were the intentions (approved by the publishers) respecting the new work, the illustrations for which were to be woodcuts provided by George Cattermole, D. Maclise, R.A., and Hablôt K. Browne ("Phiz"). Dickens could not at first satisfy himself as to the title of his forthcoming production, and in his private Diary we find him hesitating between "Old Humphrey's Clock" and "Master Humphrey's Clock." In a note to Mr. Forster he said: "I am thinking awfully, but not writing, as I intend (please God) to start to-morrow. I incline rather more to Master Humphrey's Clock than Old Humphrey's—if so be there is no danger of the pensive confounding 'Master' with a boy." Presently he intimates that he has determined on the final title, "or something very near it," and continues: "I have a notion of this old file in the queer house, opening the book by an account of himself, and, among other peculiarities, of his affection for an old quaint queer-cased clock," and that in the clock-case he should keep odd manuscripts, to be read aloud at the meetings of a club named after the ancient timepiece. Two days afterwards he began "Master Humphrey," and a week later he finished the first number.

In one of Dickens's minor writings of this period ("Sketches of Young Couples") appeared an advertisement of the new work, which was thus announced: "Now wound up and going, preparatory to its striking on Saturday, the 28th March, Master Humphrey's Clock, maker's name—'Boz.' The Figures and Hands by George Cattermole, Esq., and 'Phiz.'" It was to be "published every Saturday morning, price 3*d.*," and the announcement thus continues:—

"Master Humphrey hopes (and is almost tempted to believe) that all degrees of readers, young or old, rich or poor, sad or merry, easy of amusement or difficult to entertain, may find something agreeable in the face of his old Clock. That, when they have made its acquaintance, its voice may sound cheerfully in their ears, and be suggestive of none but pleasant thoughts. That they may come to have favourite and familiar associations connected with its name, and to look for it as for a welcome friend.

"From week to week, then, MASTER HUMPHREY will set his Clock, trusting that while it counts the hours, it will sometimes cheat them of their heaviness, and that while it marks the tread of Time, it will scatter a few slight flowers on the Old Mower's path.

"Until the specified period arrives, and he can enter freely upon that confidence with his readers which he is impatient to maintain, he may only bid them a short farewell, and look forward to their next meeting."

Much has been said concerning the origin of the title "Master Humphrey's Clock." Dr. Charles Rogers (editor of "The Modern Scottish Minstrel") has recorded * that in 1864 he called upon a watchmaker named Humphrey[s] at Barnard Castle, Durham, to ask if he had been correctly informed respecting Dickens's title having been suggested by the clock in front of his shop. The worthy horologist replied in the affirmative, and declared that he possessed a letter from the novelist corroborating this, to-

* *Daily News*, July, 1870.

gether with a copy of the work inscribed by his own hand. He further stated that he became acquainted with Dickens in 1838, through his going across to the shop from the hotel, and asking him for information about the state of the neighbouring boarding-schools, concerning which he was then writing something for "Nicholas Nickleby." In a biographical sketch of William Humphreys,* a clockmaker of Barnard Castle, we learn that in 1828, when about sixteen years of age, he commenced to make the identical timepiece which afterwards became famous as Master Humphrey's Clock, and of which a minute description is given. On its completion the following year it was placed just inside the shop door; but in 1838, when (shortly after Dickens's visit) Humphreys migrated to Old Hartlepool, it accompanied him, and remained in his possession until his death.† The original clock (the authenticity of which has been vouched for by many), as well

* *Monthly Chronicle* (Newcastle-on-Tyne), November, 1887.

† William Humphreys died suddenly at Stranton, West Hartlepool, in 1887, aged seventy-five, having been born during the same year as Dickens. In his latter days he delighted in referring to his association with the great novelist.

as a copy of it, was exhibited at the Newcastle Jubilee Exhibition in 1887.

The first number of "Master Humphrey's Clock" appeared on April 4th, 1840, and nearly seventy thousand copies were sold. The critics did not favour the new form of publication—a kind of serial miscellany of tales and sketches—so that the circulation began to decrease; but it recovered when Dickens revived Mr. Pickwick and the Wellers, many of whose quaint sayings are to be found here. The construction of "Master Humphrey's Clock" was considered, however, to be inartistic; therefore the novelist speedily dropped the idea he once entertained of enlisting the services of other writers, and abandoned the plan of having an upstairs club round the Clock, as well as a similar social gathering downstairs under the name of "Mr. Weller's Watch." The cumbrous machinery disposed of, Dickens began seriously to work upon a continuous story—that of the old curiosity-dealer and his grandchild—which began in the fourth number. On its conclusion, it was followed by that more dramatic romance, "Barnaby Rudge," both of these tales originally appearing in "Master Humphrey's Clock."

During the progress of the publication,

certain ambitious persons, mistaking it for a kind of *omnium gatherum*, proffered contributions to its pages, and the author was compelled to issue this notification, which was printed on the wrappers of some of the weekly numbers:—

"MASTER HUMPHREY'S CLOCK.

"Mr. Dickens begs to inform all those Ladies and Gentlemen who have tendered him contributions for this work, and all those who may now or at any future time have it in contemplation to do so, that he cannot avail himself of their obliging offers, as it is written solely by himself, and cannot possibly include any productions from other hands.

"This announcement will serve for a final answer to all correspondents, and will render any private communications unnecessary."

"THE OLD CURIOSITY SHOP."

Dickens could not immediately decide upon a suitable designation for his new story. On March 4th, 1840, he wrote to Mr. Forster: "What do you think of the following double title for the beginning of that little tale? 'PERSONAL ADVENTURES OF MASTER HUMPHREY: THE OLD CURIOSITY SHOP.' I have thought of 'Master Humphrey's Tale,' 'Master Humphrey's Narrative,' 'A Passage in

Master Humphrey's Life,' but I 'don't think any does so well as this. I have also thought of THE OLD CURIOSITY DEALER AND THE CHILD instead of THE OLD CURIOSITY SHOP. . . ." The title selected by Dickens and approved by Mr. Forster has been objected to because there is scarcely anything in the book about old curiosities, while the bric-à-brac shop itself disappears from the scene in the early chapters.

The story, as it developed, became remarkable both for humour and pathos. Its popularity increased accordingly, and reached its height when the child-heroine, Little Nell, appeared on the scene, the sale of the particular numbers in which the young girl figures attaining to nearly a hundred thousand copies. It was early in 1840, during a birthday visit to Walter Savage Landor, then lodging at St. James's Square, Bath, that the fancy which led to the creation of Little Nell first dawned upon the novelist, whose original intention was to utilise it only for a short story. No character in prose fiction was a greater favourite with Landor; one day, years after the tale was published, he burst out with a tremendous emphasis and declared that the mistake of his life was that he had not purchased the house in Bath, and then and there burned it to the ground, so that no meaner association should ever desecrate her birthplace. The genial Thomas Hood wrote eloquently in praise of this almost divine creature—an essay which Dickens acknowledged as having read with "an unusual glow of pleasure and encouragement." Sara Coleridge, while incorrectly assuming the idea to be a good deal borrowed from "Wilhelm Meister," admired Nell exceedingly, considering her a far purer, lovelier, more *English* conception than Mignon. The novelist himself was greatly wrapped up in this pathetic character, for the reason that in her he had enshrined the memory of his sister-in-law, Mary Hogarth, whose premature death so sadly affected him. Dickens assured his friends that Little Nell was an object of his love, that he mourned her loss for a month after her death, and felt as if one of his own offspring had left a vacant chair.

Little Nell's traits of character obtained so great a hold upon the public mind that Dickens received many anonymous requests imploring him "not to kill" her. He had, however, been so advised by Mr. Forster, for, as the novelist himself agreed, it would destroy the sentiment of the conception if the child lived to end her days in a prosaic manner. The death of Little Nell touched a very tender chord in every heart. Even men like Daniel O'Connell were overcome by its pathos, and it is recorded of the great Irish agitator that, on reading the account of the sad incident, his eyes filled with tears, as, with a sigh, he said: "He should not have killed her! He should not have killed her! She was too good!" Being unable to read more, he indignantly threw the book out of window. From the remote wilds of America the novelist received letters referring to the loss of children, the sorrowing parents numbering his little heroine with their household gods, "and so" [observed the author] "pouring out their trials and sources of comfort in them, before me, as a friend, that I have been inexpressibly moved, and am whenever I think of them."* That stern critic, Lord Jeffrey (concerning whom Carlyle remarked that "he said more brilliant and interesting things than any man he had met in the world"), was entirely overcome by the pathetic description of Nell's death, and was discovered in his library

* *Vide* Letter to Mr. L. Gaylord Clark, dated September 28th, 1841.

sobbing terribly. Macready, too, who begged Dickens to spare her life, was grievously affected by the tragic ending of the story. Mr. Forster states that he never knew the author wind up a tale with such sorrowful reluctance, availing himself of any excuse to postpone the conclusion. He confessed to his future biographer that he could not sleep at nights through thinking of the child; just before the end he declared himself to be "the wretchedest of the wretched," that no one would miss the child as he should, after her death,—and therefore he lingered over the sad finale. To the Rev. William Harness he wrote, declining an invitation to dinner: "The finishing of 'The Old Curiosity Shop' is such a painful task to me that I must concentrate myself upon it tooth and nail, and go out nowhere until it is done"; and George Cattermole, the artist, received a similar communication: "I am breaking my heart over this story, and cannot bear to finish it."

"The Old Curiosity Shop" was completed on January 17th, 1841, at four o'clock in the morning. "It makes me very melancholy," he remarked to Mr. Forster, "to think that all these people are lost to me for ever, and I feel as if I never could become attached to any new set of characters." When published in book form it proved an extraordinary success, and, especially in America, greatly increased the author's fame. Washington Irving was deeply touched by its "exquisite and sustained pathos, so deep, but so pure and healthy," and considered that the whole of the story was characterised by "a moral sublimity and beauty wrought out with matchless simplicity of fancies . . . that leaves me at a loss how sufficiently to express my admiration." Caroline Fox wrote (February 18th, 1841): "I am exceedingly enjoying Boz's 'Master Humphrey's Clock,' which is still in progress. That man is carrying out Carlyle's work more emphatically than any; he forces the sympathies of all into unwonted channels, and teaches us that Punch and Judy men, beggar children, and daft old men are also of our species, and are not, more than ourselves, removed from the sphere of the heroic. He is doing a world of good in a very healthy way."* Of the many tributes the story has received, none is more pleasing than the delightful verses by Mr. Bret Harte, entitled "Dickens in Camp"—a *tour de*

* *Vide* "Journals of Caroline Fox," 1883.

force—"hastily but honestly written" on the day that the news of the death of the "Master" was telegraphed to him at San Rafael, California, while the last sheets of the July *Overland* monthly magazine were going to press. These sympathetic lines (since included in Mr. Bret Harte's collected Poems) describe the reading aloud, by a rough Californian miner to his comrades around their camp fire, of "The Old Curiosity Shop."

A quaint red-tiled building with plaster front, situated in Portsmouth Street, Lincoln's Inn Fields (and supposed to have been the dairy, two centuries ago, of the Duchess of Portsmouth, who pastured her cows in the adjacent meadows), has been pointed out as the actual house which Dickens described as the home of Nelly and her grandfather, for which reason it has attracted crowds of visitors from all parts of the civilised world;* especially was this the case when, a few years ago, the ancient structure was threatened with

* Dickens, in his story, located the Curiosity Shop within the City boundary, and referred to it at the time as having been long demolished to allow of street improvements. The house in Portsmouth Street is still standing, but there is no reason whatever for supposing that it has anything to do with the home of Little Nell.

destruction, the locality then being besieged from morning till night by worshippers at the hypothetical shrine of Little Nell. The picturesque old church in which the child was buried has been identified at Tong, in Shropshire; it certainly corresponds somewhat with Dickens's description and Cattermole's illustration.

The prototype of the Marchioness was an orphan from the Chatham workhouse, and the novelist took his first impression of her when she lived, as a maid-of-all-work, with the Dickens's family in Bayham Street, Camden Town. It was at the same time that he met an elderly couple and their only son, whom he introduced in his story as the Garland family, and with whom he lodged in Lant Street, Borough, during the sad period when his parents were incarcerated in the Marshalsea—the same street, indeed, where Bob Sawyer (of "Pickwick" renown) also resided many years afterwards.

The original MS. of "The Old Curiosity Shop" is in the South Kensington Museum. Mr. J. F. Dexter possesses some of the "galley" proofs of the story, which are specially interesting for the reason that they prove Dickens to have occasionally supplied more "copy" than was required for the particular number on hand. At the top of one slip the printer has written, "There is a page and half too much here," and accordingly Dickens deleted whole paragraphs, one of which is very lengthy. In his later works there was frequently a want of sufficient "copy."

"Barnaby Rudge."

The wrapper of No. 41 of "Master Humphrey's Clock" (dated January 9th, 1841), besides notifying that "Barnaby Rudge" would commence immediately upon the completion of "The Old Curiosity Shop," contained the statement that the former story was originally projected with a view to its separate publication in another and much more expensive form. This was the work which was repeatedly announced by Macrone, and thus advertised at the end of the Second Series of "Sketches by Boz": "A new novel by Boz. Gabriel Vardon, by Charles Dickens, Esq., author of 'Sketches by Boz,' 'The Pickwick Papers,' etc. Three volumes, post octavo." There is no reference to it by name in Mr. Forster's biography, but in a letter from Dickens to Macrone we read that the author agreed to accept the sum of £200 "for the first edition of a work of fiction (in three volumes of the usual type) to be written by me, and to be entitled 'Gabriel Vardon, the Locksmith of London,' of which not more than one thousand copies are to be printed." But owing to stress of work the writing of "Barnaby Rudge," as the tale was subsequently designated, was deferred *sine die*, being eventually fated to succeed "The Old Curiosity Shop." The latter, completed in seventy-three chapters, was immediately followed by a short chapter of Master Humphrey's Reflections, after which (in the 46th number, dated February 13th, 1841) began the new story, which was not interrupted at all. In it appears Gabriel Varden (not Vardon), a locksmith, which indicates a connection with the romance first heralded by Macrone a few years previously.

It was intended that "Barnaby Rudge" should follow "Oliver Twist" as a serial in *Bentley's Miscellany*, and then be published in three volumes; but, owing to certain disputes respecting financial arrangements, the novelist's relations with Bentley became somewhat strained, and the project was abandoned. In the meantime Dickens had entered into an agreement with Messrs. Chapman and Hall regarding the publication of "Pickwick," the terms of which ensured for the author much higher remuneration than he had hitherto received, and this caused him to be dissatisfied with the comparatively modest sum it was at first arranged he should be paid for "Barnaby." This sum (Mr. Percy Fitzgerald tells us) was originally £500, but in a subsequent agreement the price named for the story was £2,000, with an additional £1,000 if the sale exceeded ten thousand copies, and a final sum of £1,000 more if the sale exceeded fifteen thousand. Dickens refused this generous offer, and, Bentley magnanimously releasing him from the agreement, fresh arrangements were made with Messrs. Chapman and Hall, in May, 1840, they consenting to pay him £50 a week for "Master Humphrey's Clock," irrespective of success or failure, and to defray all cost of printing, advertising, and illustration. Dickens was held pecuniarily responsible for whatever literary assistance he required; he was also allowed one half of the entire profits on each number, not deducting the expenses.* The publishers bound themselves to issue the work on these terms for twelve months certain; and Dickens was prepared to go on for five years if they elected that the publication should be continued so long. At the expiration of the agreement the copyright and stock on hand were to be equally shared between the parties.

In 1838 Dickens had the story much in his mind, but the writing of it was not actually commenced until the autumn of the following year. From that time until its conclusion he frequently informed Mr. Forster of the progress he made with it, as indicated by the following quotations from his letters: "Thank God, all goes famously. I have worked at 'Barnaby' all day."—"'Barnaby' moves, not at race-horse speed."—"All well. 'Barnaby' has reached his tenth page." A considerable interval elapsed before he again tackled the story, and in January, 1841, he says: "I didn't stir out yesterday, but sat and *thought* all day; not writing a

* *Vide* Letter from Dickens to Mr. Thomas Mitton, his solicitor; dated July 20th, 1839. The Agreement here referred to sold for £16 10*s.* in 1891—a small sum when it is remembered how seldom such a document comes to the hammer.

line; not so much as the cross of a *t* or dot of an *i.* I imaged forth a good deal of 'Barnaby' by keeping my mind steadily on him; and am happy to say I have gone to work this morning in good twig, strong hope, and cheerful spirits." On February 25th, he wrote: "I have (it's four o'clock) done a very fair morning's work, at which I have sat very close, and been blessed besides with a clear view of the end of the volume;" and two months later, "I am getting on very slowly. I want to stick to the story; and the fear of committing myself, because of the impossibility of trying back or altering a syllable, makes it much harder than it looks. . . ." On August 5th, he remarked: "I am warming up very much about 'Barnaby.' Oh! if I only had him from this time to the end, in monthly numbers;"—for he felt more than ever, during the closing scenes, the constraints of weekly publication. Writing six days later, he said: "I was always sure I could make a good thing of 'Barnaby,' and I think you will find that it comes out strong to the last word. . . . I am in great heart and spirits with the story." A serious illness then harassed him; but he bore up gallantly, and on October 22nd (while still in his sick-room), he wrote,

"I hope I sha'n't leave off any more, now, until I have finished 'Barnaby.'" On November 2nd, the printers received the final chapters.

In the Preface to "Barnaby Rudge" the author explains that he was induced to write this romance by the fact that no account of the famous Gordon Riots of 1780 had been, to his knowledge, presented in any work of fiction, and that the subject comprised very extraordinary and remarkable incidents. He gathered his materials for this powerful description principally from the files of old newspapers in the British Museum. Respecting this feature of the book, Edgar Allan Poe maintained that the introduction of the Riots was altogether an afterthought. "It is evident," he said, "that they have no necessary connection with the story. The whole events of the drama would have proceeded as well without as with them. They have even the appearance of being *forcibly* introduced. All the characters, at a certain point, are thrown forward for a period of five years . . . for no more plausible reason than to afford an opportunity of describing the 'No Popery' Riots."*

* "The Literati," etc. By Edgar A. Poe. New York, 1850.

Mr. Forster mentions that Dickens conceived the notion of including, amongst the actors in the Riots, "three splendid fellows, who should order, lead, control, and be obeyed as natural guides of the crowd in that delirious time, and who should turn out, when all was over, to have broken out of Bedlam"; but he abandoned this intention at his friend's instigation, the conception being, perhaps, too audacious for what purported to be a substantially historical treatment of his theme. This was evidently the subject to which Mr. Wilkie Collins alluded when, writing in his marked copy of Mr. Forster's biography, he said: "Where is the unsoundness of it? I call it a fine idea. New, powerful, highly dramatic, and well within the limits of truth to nature. It would have greatly improved the weakest book that Dickens ever wrote."

It is recorded that the prototype of Barnaby Rudge recently died at the age of sixty-eight. He was a peculiarly eccentric young man named Walter de Brisac, who lived at Chatham—a pedlar by profession. When Dickens's attention was first drawn to him he was wearing a suit of clothes suggestive of a remote period of antiquity, and was clad in the same garments when he died, suffering from wretchedness and destitution. His father is reported to have held a commission in the British Army. Lord George Gordon, the hero of the Riots, was of course the veritable Scottish lord, the second son of Cosmo, third Duke of Gordon; proclaiming himself to be "a friend of the people," he instituted public meetings in support of the Protestant interest, which culminated in serious riots, the cry of "No Popery" being the only guarantee of security from violence at the hands of the mob. In describing Sir John Chester, Dickens evidently had in his mind the worldly Lord Chesterfield—a prototype much more in harmony with Sir John than was Sir William Maule, one of the Justices of the Court of Common Pleas, who (says Dr. Shelton Mackenzie) was supposed to have stood for the portrait.

That poor Barnaby's raven, the redoubtable Grip who plays so important a part in the tale, is drawn from life, we have the novelist's assurance. He states in the Preface to the first Cheap Edition that this famous bird is a compound of two great originals, of whom he was at different times the proud possessor; and he gives an amusing account of their various idiosyncrasies, many of which were conspicuous in Barnaby's feathered friend. Dickens's first raven (also named Grip) poisoned himself with white lead; the second, who died from unknown causes, kept "his eye to the last upon the meat as it roasted, and suddenly turned over on his back with a sepulchral cry of 'Cuckoo.'"* Charles Dickens's fondness for these pets induced a punning friend to remark that he was "raven mad," which gave rise to an absurd rumour that he was insane and confined in a lunatic asylum. Grip, at his death, was stuffed and placed in a glass case, and his subsequent appearance in the auction-room, at the sale of the novelist's treasures and effects, was hailed with rapturous cheers—a striking tribute to the genius of him who had immortalised the bird in the story. Grip was purchased, after keen competition, for one hundred and twenty guineas, amidst tumultuous applause, the purchasers being the London Stereoscopic Company. Professor Ward

* A letter from Dickens to his friend Angus Fletcher, describing the illness and death of Grip, recently changed hands at Sotheby's sale-rooms for £15 10*s*. Shortly afterwards the sum of £50 was offered, and refused, merely for the right to reproduce in an American journal a *facsimile* of this interesting epistle.

has suggested that Dickens may have derived the first notion of Grip from the raven Ralpho—likewise the property of an idiot —who frightened Roderick Random and Strap out of their wits, and into the belief that he *was* the personage Grip so persistently declared himself to be [*vide* "Roderick Random," Chap. XIII.]. This is not improbable, remembering how Dickens, as a boy, revelled in the works of Smollett and Fielding.

* * * * *

Dickens's intention to wind up the "Clock" (that is, in the sense of discontinuing it) was intimated on the wrapper of No. 80 (October 9th, 1841), eight weeks before the work was brought to a close. "Barnaby Rudge" finished with its eighty-second chapter, and the book concluded with a paper of six pages from Master Humphrey. The unsold stock of "Master Humphrey's Clock" was, soon after completion, divested of the introductory, intercalary, and concluding chapters, miscellaneous papers, etc.,* and "The Old Curiosity Shop" and "Barnaby Rudge" issued as independent stories,

* These were reproduced as the "Other Stories" forming, with "Edwin Drood," a volume in the 1867, 1871, and 1873 editions of Dickens's works.

at thirteen shillings each. Subsequently these were published in demy octavo, uniform with the author's chief works, having all the original woodcuts. "Master Humphrey's Clock" was dedicated to Samuel Rogers, the banker-poet, to whom Dickens acknowledged indebtedness for "a beautiful thought" in the last chapter but one of "The Old Curiosity Shop," which is taken from "Ginevra," and has reference to "an old man wandering *as in quest of something.*"

"Master Humphrey's Clock" was issued in eighty-eight weekly numbers, imperial octavo (white wrappers), at 3*d.* each, commencing April 4th, 1840, and closing November 27th, 1841; and in twenty monthly parts (green wrappers), the price of each part varying from 1*s.* to 1*s.* 3*d.*, this depending upon the amount of text in the number. The whole constituted three volumes, of which Vol. I. contains pp. vi. (including page with Dedication and one blank page), and pp. 306; Vol. II., pp. vi., 306; and Vol. III., pp. vi., 426. They were published (1840-41) by Messrs. Chapman and Hall in cloth, cut edges, at £1 6*s.* 6*d.* Instead of etchings, as in previous works, the illustrations were engraved on wood. These were drawn by George Cattermole and Hablôt

6

K. Browne, with the exception of one by Samuel Williams (Vol. I., p. 46), and one by D. Maclise, R.A. (Vol. II., p. 108). Dickens was so delighted with Cattermole's drawings that, when thanking him for his invaluable co-operation, he said it was the first time any designs for what he had written had touched and moved him, and caused him to feel that they expressed the idea he had in his mind.

The first Cheap Edition of "The Old Curiosity Shop" appeared in 1848, and of "Barnaby Rudge" in 1849; these contained new Prefaces, with frontispieces by Cattermole and Browne respectively.

The original manuscript of "Barnaby Rudge" is at South Kensington. A copy of "Master Humphrey's Clock" in the original weekly numbers is valued at from £4 to £5.

"MARTIN CHUZZLEWIT."

BEFORE the termination of "Master Humphrey's Clock" in November, 1841, Dickens had arranged with Messrs. Chapman and Hall for another story in shilling numbers, which, however, was not to be commenced until twelve months later. The public were informed of the proposed venture in an Address by the novelist, printed on the wrapper of No. 80 of "Master Humphrey's Clock," where he said: "Taking advantage of the respite which the close of this work will afford me, I have decided, in January next, to pay a visit to America. . . . On the first of November eighteen hundred and forty-two I purpose, if it please God, to commence my book in monthly parts, under the old green cover, in the old size and form, and at the old price." This book was "Martin Chuzzlewit."

It was not until November 12th, 1842,

that Mr. Forster received from Dickens the title of the new tale; "Don't lose it," he said, "for I have no copy." On the Christian name of his hero he determined at once, but the surname formed the subject of considerable discussion, the respective merits of Sweezleden, Sweezleback, Sweezlewag, Chuzzletoe, Chuzzleboy, Chubblewig, and Chuzzlewig being duly considered before that of Chuzzlewit was adopted. The full title, as it originally appeared, was lengthy and elaborate, and read thus:—

"The Life and Adventures of Martin Chuzzlewit, His Relatives, Friends, and Enemies. Comprising all his Wills and his Ways; with an Historical Record of What he Did, and What he Didn't: Showing, moreover, Who inherited the Family Plate, Who came in for the Silver Spoons, and Who for the Wooden Ladles. The Whole forming a Complete Key to the House of Chuzzlewit. Edited by 'Boz.' With Illustrations by 'Phiz.'"

In subsequent editions the book was simply called "Martin Chuzzlewit."

"American Notes" (published in October, 1842) greatly excited public opinion across the Atlantic, owing to the author's strongly expressed observations on the more pronounced manners and customs of the country. In "Chuzzlewit" he made more free and dashing use of his American observations than he had done in the previous work, and thereby redoubled the anger felt against him in the United States.* The strictures of Transatlantic critics so incensed him that in revenge he altered the very structure of "Martin Chuzzlewit" before he had written much of the story, and carried his hero to America by a very improbable method, in order to obtain an opportunity of further revealing to his readers "the ludicrous side of the American character." Although this was not ill-naturedly done, the Americans continued to execrate him for some considerable time, and he tells in one of his letters (comically, but with a good deal of earnestness too) how three or four years afterwards, meeting some Americans

* Carlyle, after reading the first volume of Mr. Forster's Life of Dickens, said: "Me nothing in it so surprises as these two American explosions around poor Dickens, *all* Yankee-doodle-dom, blazing up like one universal soda-water bottle round so very measurable a phenomenon; this and the way the phenomenon takes it was curiously and even genially interesting to me, and significant of Yankee-doodle-dom." *Vide* "Conversations with Carlyle," by Sir Charles Gavan Duffy, K.C.M.G., 1892.

on a ship in the Mediterranean, he was in terror, from their manner, of their throwing him overboard. Happily, any ill-feeling thus engendered was soon obliterated, for the sensitiveness of American patriotism (as a friend of Mark Twain informed the present writer) did not brood over the "Notes" and the chapters in "Chuzzlewit" long enough "to seriously interfere with the tender regard and enthusiastic admiration which the genius of his literature had kindled in the universal heart."

Dickens, at first, had some idea of opening this romance in the lantern of a lighthouse, but this intention was abandoned. The real origin of the book, as Mr. Forster affirms, was the notion of taking Pecksniff for a type of character; while Dickens himself tells us (in the Preface to the first Cheap Edition, 1849) that his object was "to show how Selfishness propagates itself, and to what a grim giant it may grow from small beginnings." In a word, "Chuzzlewit" may be considered as a crusade against "cant" in its most vicious form. Writing to Professor Felton (December 31st, 1842), he said: "I have been hard at work on my new book, of which the first number has just appeared. . . . I particularly commend, my dear Felton, one Mr. Pecksniff and his daughters to your tender regards. I have a kind of liking for them myself." To the same friend he wrote, some two months later: "I am in great health and spirits, and powdering away at 'Chuzzlewit,' with all manner of facetiousness rising up before me as I go on." The nitial number was dated January, 1843, and the publication ran on uninterruptedly until its conclusion in July, 1844. The uncertainty with respect to the construction of the story (which proved, as Mr. Forster affirmed, defective) caused Dickens much concern, "beginning so hurriedly as at last he did," says his biographer, "altering his course at the opening, and seeing little of the main track of his design." "Chuzzlewit," in the matter of its sale as a serial, was at first a comparative failure, the average number per month never exceeding twenty-three thousand copies, as against more than double that of previous novels. This result, for which many reasons have been assigned, caused the author much disappointment, for, as he wrote to Mr. Forster when the work was nearly finished, he thought it, in a hundred points, immeasurably the best of his stories. In volume form, however, the demand became very great, ranking fairly well with "Pickwick" and "Copperfield," the half-year's profits amounting to £750.

It had been agreed that, during the twelve months' interval before the book began, the novelist was to be paid £150 each month; but this was to be drawn from his share of the profits, and in no way to interfere with the monthly payments of £200 while the story was running, that sum to be accounted as part of the expenses, for all of which, and all risks incident, the publishers made themselves responsible, under conditions the same as in the "Master Humphrey's Clock" agreement; except that, out of the profits of each number, they were to have only a fourth, three-fourths going to the author, and this arrangement was to hold good until the termination of six months after the completion of the book, when, on payment to Dickens of a fourth of the value of all existing stock, the publishers were to have half the future interest.

Not only did the diminished sale of "Chuzzlewit" as a serial create disappointment, but, in combination with other vexations of a pecuniary nature, it led to a temporary severance of the hitherto friendly relations existing between author and publishers. A clause had been inserted in the agreement to the effect that, in the case of the book not proving remunerative, £50 of the £200 stipulated to be paid monthly might be withheld; and on one of the partners hinting (on the eve of issuing the seventh number) that the condition was likely to be enforced, Dickens became wroth, and conceived a sentiment of revenge against Messrs. Chapman and Hall, who had secured certain shares in the venture. So keen was his irritation that a parting became inevitable, and the novelist intimated that his publishing relations with them would close with the conclusion of "Chuzzlewit." After this, negotiations were opened with Messrs. Bradbury and Evans, the printers, which resulted in an agreement under which, in consideration of an advance of £2,800, Dickens assigned to them a fourth share in whatever he might write during the ensuing eight years.

The American scenes in "Chuzzlewit" were generally considered at the time as gross caricatures, about which the Americans were morbidly sensitive. No sooner had the book reached Transatlantic shores than their indignation was renewed with great violence, and some of the critics seemed to be (as Dickens expressed it) "stark, staring, raving mad." It is amusing to learn that at the Boston Theatre, New York—the burlesque of "Macbeth" being performed—all sorts of worthless articles (Mexican rifles, Pennsylvanian bonds, etc.) were pitched into the witches' cauldron, in the incantation scene, but nothing provoked louder cheers than when the last work by "Boz" was thrown in! Certain American critics, however, are candid enough to admit the accuracy of Dickens's strictures. One of them looks upon the sketches in "Chuzzlewit" as being among the cleverest and truest things he has ever written, and considers that "the satire was richly deserved, well applied, and has done a great deal of good. To claim that it was mere burlesque and exaggeration is sheer nonsense, and it is highly disingenuous to deny the existence of the absurdities upon which it was founded."* Another American writer, the late Miss Kate Field, says: "As for certain American portraits painted in 'Martin Chuzzlewit,' I should as soon think of objecting to them as I should think of objecting to any other discovery in natural history."

* *Vide* Introduction to "Speeches of Charles Dickens," edited by R. H. Shepherd, 1884.

That the novelist's descriptions of American scenery were founded on fact is proved, in one instance at least, by the identification of the locality known as "Eden" in the story, which was found to exist somewhere between Harrisburgh and Pittsburgh on the journey over the Alleghany Mountains, as described in the "Notes"; public opinion points to the city of Cairo on the Mississippi River as the actual spot. As already stated, American anger was short-lived, and a friendly feeling between Dickens and his Transatlantic readers was restored long before his second visit to the United States (1867-8), on which occasion the novelist, in an admirable speech delivered by him at a dinner given in his honour at New York, remarked upon the beneficial changes, moral and physical, he then observed in the country.

> "This testimony," he said, "so long as I live, and so long as my descendants have any right in my books, I shall cause to be republished as an appendix to every copy of those two books of mine ["Martin Chuzzlewit" and "American Notes"] in which I have referred to America. And this I will do and cause to be done, not in mere love and thankfulness, but because I regard it as an act of plain justice and honour."

When this postscript (dated "May,

1868") was appended to both the above works in the "Charles Dickens" and subsequent editions, the author added the following:—

> "I said these words with the greatest earnestness that I could lay upon them, and I repeat them in print here with equal earnestness. So long as this book shall last, I hope that they will form a part of it, and will be fairly read as inseparable from my experiences and impressions of America."

"Phiz's" portrait of Mr. Pecksniff (who has been described as the English Tartuffe) suggested a resemblance to Sir Robert Peel—indeed, the eminent statesman was often made to pose pictorially in the contemporary pages of *Punch* as that famous Dickens character. It is said that when Mr. Samuel Carter Hall (editor of the *Art Journal* and founder of the *Art Union*) went to lecture in the United States, he was awkwardly heralded by the American press as the prototype of Pecksniff; *Punch* also referred to him as Pecksniff, and to the *Art Union* as the "Pecksniffery," whereupon Mr. Hall threatened a libel action, which created a bad impression at the time. His sententious catch-phrase of appealing to "hand, head, and heart" was always made the most of, and *Punch* delighted in paraphrasing it as "gloves, hat, and waistcoat."* In a letter (1844) to Mr. R. J. Lane, A.R.A., Dickens wrote that a great many people (particularly those who might have sat for the character) considered even Mr. Pecksniff a grotesque impossibility. At Alderbury, two miles from Salisbury, there is a house called "St. Mary's Grange," which has been pointed out as the Pecksniffian residence, where can be seen the turret whence his young men were supposed to prepare his "elevations" of the cathedral.

That notorious personage, Sarah Gamp, is rightly considered as one of the most remarkable instances of humorous portraiture to be found in English literature; indeed, a certain critic favourably compared this creation with that of Juliet's nurse, and averred that "Mrs. Gamp is the greater of the two."† Mrs. Gamp and her friend Betsey Prig are true specimens of the ordinary sick-nurse of the period, the former being a portrait of a person hired by a distinguished friend of the novelist, a lady, to take charge of an invalid very dear to her; a common habit

* *Vide* "History of *Punch*," by M. H. Spielmann, 1895.

† *Spectator*, June 11th, 1870.

of this nurse in the sick-room, among other Gampish peculiarities, was to rub her nose along the top of the tall fender. To these uncultured women the trained nurse of to-day affords a welcome contrast, thanks to the revelations in "Martin Chuzzlewit." It appears that Dickens's conception of the character of Mrs. Gamp was not entirely original, for it has been pointed out that her habit of placing certain refreshment within easy reach finds a parallel in Homer's "Odyssey," viii. 70, where are described in almost the very same words the arrangements made for the comfort of the bard Democritus.

In 1847, Dickens entertained the idea of reviving Mrs. Gamp by writing in her peculiar vernacular a little *jeu d'esprit* in the form of a history of a theatrical tour in the Provinces, undertaken by himself and friends to raise a fund for the benefit of Leigh Hunt. It was to be, in the phraseology of that extraordinary character, a new "Piljian's Projiss," and published with illustrations by the artist-members of this famous company, in aid of the fund. The project, however, perished prematurely, but the proposed letterpress was printed by Mr. Forster in his biography of the novelist.

"Martin Chuzzlewit" was issued in

twenty shilling numbers (each in a green wrapper), commencing in January, 1843, and ending in July, 1844, Parts 19 and 20 forming a double number. It was published complete in one volume, cloth, at one guinea—pp. xiv., one unnumbered page of Errata, and pp. 624—with a Preface dated "London, June 25, 1844," and a Dedication to Miss Burdett-Coutts. There are forty illustrations by "Phiz," including an illustrated title-page; the latter, in its first state, contains an error in the misplacing of the £ sign after the figures 100 on the way-post, which is only to be found in a few of the earliest copies. The story has often been re-issued in the same form, in green cloth, either with or without a date. The first Cheap Edition, with a new Preface dated "London, November, 1849," was published in that year, with a frontispiece by F. Stone, A.R.A.

The price of a first edition of "Martin Chuzzlewit," in blue cloth as issued, is from £3 to £5; it is scarce in the original parts, but rarely sells in that state for more than £5, not being popular with collectors for some reason, although copies containing the error on the etched title-page (the number of which is extremely limited) are naturally much in request. In the concluding chapters of the MS. of "Martin Chuzzlewit," which is at South Kensington, the author's greater pains and elaboration of writing first become very obvious.

"DOMBEY AND SON."

CHARLES DICKENS entered upon his sixth great novel in the pretty little villa of Rosemont, at Lausanne, Switzerland. He announced the interesting fact to Mr. Forster in a letter dated June 28th, 1846: "I performed the feat yesterday—only wrote the first slip—but there it is, and it is a plunge straight over head and ears into the story." At the same time the author referred to an odd coincidence, which is somewhat indicative of his inherent belief in the superstitious. While unpacking a box he withdrew a volume, and said, "Now, whatever passage my thumb rests on I shall take as having reference to my work"; it was "Tristram Shandy," and he opened it at these words: "What a book it is likely to turn out! Let us begin it." So, encouraged by such a favourable augury, he commenced to write "Dombey and Son."

Dickens, in the quietude of his temporary home in Switzerland, made steady progress with the new story, but at times he suffered greatly from an "extraordinary nervousness" that would come upon him after he had been at his desk all day. On July 12th he indicated enthusiasm in his work by informing Mr. Forster that he thought "Dombey" very strong, "with great capacity in its leading idea; plenty of character that is likely to tell; and some rollicking facetiousness, to say nothing of pathos." He had intimated that there would be a great surprise for people at the end of the fourth number, alluding to the death of little Paul. This sad incident, however, was reserved for No. 5, which, we are told, was begun when Dickens felt "most abominably dull and stupid." "I have only written a slip," he said, "but I hope to get to work in strong earnest to-morrow." In September he complained of his extraordinary difficulty in "getting on FAST." "Invention, thank God," he remarked, "seems the easiest thing in the world; and I seem to have such a preposterous sense of the ridiculous, . . . as to be constantly requiring to restrain myself from launching into extravagances in the height of my enjoyment." He attributed this inability to make rapid progress with his book chiefly to his rural Swiss environment, and the strange effect which, as he thought, the absence of streets and of crowds of people had upon his brain; his description of this feeling is most curious, and those who knew him intimately were best able to realise how true it was. "I can't express," said the novelist, "how much I want these. It seems as if they supplied something to my brain, which it cannot bear, when busy, to lose. For a week or a fortnight I can write prodigiously in a retired place (as at Broadstairs), and a day in London sets me up again and starts me. But the toil and labour of writing day after day, without that magic lantern, is IMMENSE!! . . . *My* fingers seem disposed to stagnate without crowds about them." He also had upon his mind at this time a Christmas book, "The Battle of Life," and the worry attending the simultaneous preparation of the two stories distressed him exceedingly. He described himself as being sick, giddy, and capriciously despondent; as having bad nights, and being full of disquietude and anxiety. In fact, all the symptoms of excessive mental strain were apparent. However, "The Battle of Life" was speedily finished, when the coast again became clear for "Dombey," the third number of which was begun on October 26th and completed in about a fortnight. The writing of the story, upon which he now concentrated his attention, was continued in Paris, London, Brighton, and Broadstairs, and, apart from occasional intervals of slow progression, the work proceeded satisfactorily until its conclusion.

The first number was issued in October, 1846, the full title on the green wrapper reading thus: "Dealings with the Firm of Dombey and Son, Wholesale, Retail, and for Exportation"; but the novel was eventually known by its more concise cognomen. The sale of No. 1 greatly exceeded that of "Martin Chuzzlewit," amounting as it did to thirty-two thousand copies. So satisfactory a result was not anticipated by Dickens, who wrote: "The 'Dombey' sale is BRILLIANT. I had put before me thirty thousand as the limit of the most extreme success, saying that if we should reach that, I should be more than satisfied and happy; you will judge how happy I am." To M. Cerjat he wrote (November 27th, 1846): "'Dombey' is doing wonders. It went up, after the publication of the second number, over the thirty thousand. This is such a very large sale, so early in the story, that I begin to think it will beat all the rest." We learn from a letter written from Paris by the novelist to the Rev. E. Tagart (January 28th, 1847) that he was still suffering from "an uncommon depression of spirits, consequent on too much sitting over 'Dombey'"; to which statement he added, "You will be glad, I know, to hear that 'Dombey' is doing wonders." To Macready, who had expressed himself as well pleased with "Dombey," he wrote that the story was "evidently a great success and a great hit, thank God!" On March 31st, 1848, in a letter to his sister (Mrs. Burnett) he remarked: "'Dombey' is prodigiously triumphant, and I *believe* the end of that immortal history is tolerably good. I have taken great pains with it, and have been continually crying over the manuscript."

The description of the last scene in Paul Dombey's brief life is undoubtedly one of the most touching passages in the English language. The author himself avowed that, when "he and his little friend parted company for ever," his heart was heavy with the sorrow he had created. There were, indeed, but few of his readers who did not experience this feeling. Writing to Mr. Forster the novelist said: "Paul's death has amazed Paris. All sorts of people are open-mouthed with admiration." Thackeray, who delighted in the perusal of "Dombey" as it issued from the press, had often been heard to speak of the work in terms of the highest praise, and when he read the affecting account of the child's demise he seemed electrified at the thought that there was one man living who could exercise so complete a control over him. Putting No. 5 of "Dombey and Son" in his pocket, he hastened down to the printing-office of *Punch*, and entering the editor's room he dashed it on the table with startling vehemence, and exclaimed: "There's no writing against such power as this—one has no chance! Read that chapter describing young Paul's death: it is unsurpassed—it is stupendous!" Lord Jeffrey, absolutely overcome by its pathos, wrote to the novelist: "Oh, my dear, dear Dickens! What a No. 5 you have now given us! I have so cried and sobbed over it last night, and again this morning; and felt my heart purified by those tears, and blessed and loved you for making me shed them; and I never can bless and love you enough. Since the divine Nelly" [in "The Old Curiosity Shop"] "was found dead on her humble couch, beneath the snow and the ivy, there has been nothing like the actual dying of that sweet Paul, in the summer sunshine of that lofty room."

A careful examination of "Phiz's" design on the green wrapper discloses the fact that a great deal of the story is there foreshadowed; while a letter to Mr. Forster, which accompanied the manuscript of the first four chapters, proves conclusively that Dickens had very definite ideas as to its general plan, from which he afterwards deviated but slightly. The only important incident of the plot which appears to have been wanting in the original "stock of the soup" (as the novelist called it) was Mr. Dombey's second marriage and its consequences.

It seems probable that much of the early part of "Dombey and Son," so far as little Paul's experiences are concerned, is autobiographical, and this idea is confirmed by a letter to Mr. Forster, wherein the author writes: "I hope you will like Mrs. Pipchin's establishment. It is from the life, and I was there." The original of Mrs. Pipchin was a certain Mrs. Roylance, with whom Charles Dickens lived as a child during those troublous times when circumstances consigned him for a while to the Blacking

Warehouse. In his memoranda for the number in which Mrs. Pipchin appears are to be found the various names, beginning with that of her real prototype, out of which that finally selected was evolved: "Mrs. Roylance. . . . House at the sea-side. Mrs. Wrychin. Mrs. Tipchin. Mrs. Alchin. Mrs. Somching. Mrs. Pipchin."

It will be remembered that, under the agreement with Messrs. Bradbury and Evans, Dickens assigned to them a fourth share in whatever he might write for eight years from June 1st, 1844. This arrangement soon produced results far surpassing his expectations, for the success of "Dombey" was immediate. Referring to the book, the author said: "The profits for the half-year are brilliant. Deducting the hundred pounds a month paid six times, I have still to receive two thousand two hundred and twenty pounds, which I think is tidy." The story was completed in twenty monthly parts, at one shilling each, the last two numbers being issued together in one wrapper in April, 1848. It was then published in one volume, cloth, at one guinea—pp. xvi., one unnumbered page of *Errata*, and pp. 624—with a Preface dated "Devonshire Terrace,

Twenty-fourth March, 1848," and a Dedication to the Marchioness of Normanby. Besides the forty illustrations by Hablôt K. Browne, Messrs. Chapman and Hall subsequently issued (with Dickens's sanction) twelve additional plates, portraits of the principal characters, also designed by "Phiz."

The price of a copy of the first edition of "Dombey and Son" is from £2 to £3; if in parts, about £3. The story has frequently been issued in the same form as the first edition, with or without a date, both by Messrs. Bradbury and Evans and Messrs. Chapman and Hall. The first Cheap Edition (1858), published by the former firm, contains a frontispiece by Hablôt K. Browne and an interesting Preface, in which the author says:—

"I began this book by the Lake of Geneva, and went on with it for some months in France. The association between the writing and the place of writing is so curiously strong in my mind, that at this day, although I know every stair in the little midshipman's house, and could swear to every pew in the church in which Florence was married, or to every young gentleman's bedstead in Doctor Blimber's establishment, I yet confusedly imagine Captain Cuttle as secluding himself from Mrs. MacStinger among the mountains of Switzerland. Similarly, when I am reminded by any chance of what it was that the waves were always saying, I wander in my fancy for a whole winter night about the streets of Paris—as I really did, with a heavy heart, on the night when my little friend and I parted company for ever."

The original MS. and corrected proofs of "Dombey and Son" are at South Kensington, a few of the alterations in the latter being in the handwriting of Mr. Forster. Some critics have averred that it was inartistic to introduce little Paul Dombey and then promptly kill him; that it was Dickens's original intention to thus dispose of this pathetic figure early in the story is proved by the author's memoranda with reference to the plot, which read thus :—

Sketch of Dombey.—Mother confined with long-expected boy. *Boy born to die.* Neglected girl, Florence—a child.

Mrs. Chick—common-minded family humbug.
Wet nurse—Polly Toodle.
Toodle, a stoker.
Lots of children.
Wooden Midshipman.
Uncle—adventurous nephew—Captain Cuttle.

It is, perhaps, not generally known that

Dickens's pen-picture of Paul Dombey was inspired by the pathetic personality of a favourite nephew, Master Harry Burnett. This poor lad, who unfortunately became a cripple and died in his tenth year, resembled in many respects the little Paul of fiction; notwithstanding his affliction, he was one of the happiest and brightest of children, with a mind always marvellously active, and, especially during the last months of his short life, was full of religious sentiment, for he insisted upon having his much-thumbed Bible placed ready to his hand. There can be no doubt that the novelist, in pourtraying Mr. Dombey, had in view a particular City magnate, as he expressly wished Hablôt Browne to get a glimpse of a certain merchant, because he was "the very Dombey"—that is, externally. Carker was connected, through his father, with an eminent engineering firm, and lived in Oxford Street, where he prowled about. The original of Mrs. Skewton was recognised at the time in a Mrs. Campbell, a lady well known at Leamington; she was so tightly laced that the slightest exertion caused her to pant for breath. It is also said that her daughter stood for the second Mrs. Dombey. Captain Cuttle was one David Mainland, master of a merchantman, who was introduced to Dickens on the day when, accompanied by Thomas Chapman, Maclise, Leech, Rogers, and others, he went to see Crosby Hall, Bishopgate Street, the restoration of which had then been completed.* It is curious to read, in the first volume of the 1893 edition of his famous "Diary," that Mr. Samuel Pepys met—at the Exchange, with other Sea Commanders—Captain Cuttle. This was John Cuttle, of the *Hector*. The old nautical-instrument maker, Sol Gills, found his prototype in Mr. Norie, of the firm of Norie and Wilson, Leadenhall Street, in front of whose small shop stood the Little Wooden Midshipman, since removed to the Minories. Mr. Forster had himself some knowledge of Miss Cornelia Blimber, and Mr. Charles Dickens the Younger has stated that he was himself, "with two of Macready's boys, at a school in St. John's Wood where the master was assisted by his daughter, an amiable young lady and a thorough classical scholar—an arrangement which, in the days when the higher education of women had scarcely been heard of, seemed somewhat eccentric and first suggested the Blimber notion,

* *Vide* "Life of Charles Dickens," by R. Shelton Mackenzie [1870].

although in matters of detail there was not the slightest likeness between the two families."

That "Dombey and Son" ranked high in the opinion of its author is proved by a letter to Mr. Forster in 1849, where he wrote: "I have a strong belief that, if any of my books are read years hence, 'Dombey' will be remembered as among the best of them." He was particularly pleased on learning from a Russian man of letters, who had translated this and other of Dickens's novels into his native tongue, that "'Dombey' continued to inspire with enthusiasm the whole of literary Russia"; and that for the previous eleven years the name of the famous English author had enjoyed a wide celebrity in Russia, his works being read with avidity "from the banks of the Neva to the remotest parts of Siberia." A clever American writer, Mr. E. P. Whipple, considers that "the beauty and pathos of the work cluster around Paul and Florence, and in these exquisite creations Dickens has exceeded the previous promise of his powers." Mr. Wilkie Collins was unable to praise the story as a whole, for in his marked copy of Mr. Forster's Life of the novelist appears the following comment: "The latter half of 'Dombey' no intelligent person can have read without astonishment at the badness of it, and the disappointment that followed lowered the sale of the next book, 'Copperfield,' incomparably superior to 'Dombey' as it certainly is."

Lord Jeffrey's admiration of the touching episode of Paul Dombey's death has already been noted, and, in forecasting the tale, he said: "The Dombeys, my dear D.! how can I thank you enough for them! The truth, and the delicacy, and the softness and depth of the pathos in that opening death scene, could only come from one hand; and the exquisite taste which spares all details, and breaks off just when the effect is at its height, is wholly yours. . . ." When the final (double) number appeared, there was published in *The Sun* newspaper (April 13th, 1848) so sympathetic and earnest a review that Dickens wrote to the editor (a very unusual proceeding for him), begging him to thank the writer for his kind and appreciative criticism. The reply came from Mr. Charles Kent, the author of the review in question, and from that time dated a close friendship and constant correspondence between them.

The following incident, duly recorded by Mr. Forster, gave the novelist a sense of amused satisfaction. While the Dickens family were staying in Paris during the early days of "Dombey," his eldest son was subjected to an attack of scarlet fever, this necessitating their removal to England. The sick boy was cared for by his grandmother, Mrs. Hogarth, and, although other persons were kept out of his way for some time, his father went to see him at his lodgings. An elderly charwoman employed about the place, who had shown much sympathy in the family trouble, upon being told by Mrs. Hogarth of the approaching visit, said, "Lawk, ma'am! Is the young gentleman upstairs the son of the man who put together 'Dombey'?" Re-assured upon this point, the old dame declared she never believed it *could* be the work of one individual, and added, "Lawk, ma'am! I thought that three or four men must have put together 'Dombey'!"

"DAVID COPPERFIELD."

EARLY in 1849 Charles Dickens began to prepare the story which is universally claimed to be his masterpiece, and shares with "Pickwick" the honour of being the most popular of his novels. As in the case of "Martin Chuzzlewit," there was a difficulty at the outset in choosing a title, some of the suggestions certainly not commending themselves either in the matter of suitability or brevity. On the 23rd of February the novelist wrote to Mr. Forster: "I should like to know how the enclosed strikes you, on a first acquaintance with it. It is odd, I think, and new; but it may have A.'s difficulty of being 'too comic, my boy.' I suppose I should have to add, though, by way of motto, 'And in short it led to the very Mag's Diversions.—*Old Saying.*' Or would it be better, there being equal authority for either, 'And in short they all played Mag's Diversions.—*Old Saying*'?

"*Mag's Diversions.*

"Being the Personal History of

"Mr. Thomas Mag the Younger,

"Of Blunderstone House."

But Dickens considered this unsatisfactory, and proposed three alternative titles. The first of these was "*Mag's Diversions,* being the Personal History, Adventures, Experience, and Observation of Mr. David Mag the Younger, of Blunderstone House"; the second omitted Adventures, and Blunderstone House was called Copperfield House; while the third approached more nearly the ultimate choice, Mr. David Mag being transformed into Mr. David Copperfield the Younger and his great-aunt Margaret, although still retaining *Mag's Diversions* as its leading line.

The following tentative titles, in which the name of David Copperfield is retained and that of Mag entirely discarded, were also forwarded to Mr. Forster for careful consideration, Dickens feeling that, on the whole, he could not improve upon them :—

1. *The Copperfield Disclosures.* Being the personal history, experience, and observation,

of Mr. David Copperfield the Younger, of Blunderstone House.

2. *The Copperfield Records.* Being the personal history, experience, and observation, of Mr. David Copperfield the Younger, of Copperfield Cottage.

3. *The Last Living Speech and Confession of David Copperfield, Junior,* of Blunderstone Lodge, who was never executed at the Old Bailey. Being his personal history found among his papers.

4. *The Copperfield Survey of the World as it Rolled.* Being the personal history, experience, and observation, of Mr. David Copperfield the Younger, of Blunderstone Rookery.

5. *The Last Will and Testament of David Copperfield, the Younger,* of Blunderstone House, who was never executed at the Old Bailey. Being his personal history, adventures, and worldly experience.

6. *The Last Will and Testament of Mr. David Copperfield.* Being his personal history, which he left as a legacy.

7. *Copperfield, Complete.* Being the whole personal history and experience of Mr. David Copperfield of Blunderstone House, which he never meant to be published on any account.

"Or the opening words of No. 7 might be 'Copperfield's Entire'; and 'The Copperfield Confessions' might open Nos. 1 and 2. Now, WHAT SAY YOU?"

The cognomen "Copperfield" was evolved from Trotfield, Trotbury, Copperboy, and Copperstone. In a similar way Dickens arrived at other names in the story. For example, "Murdstone" temporarily stood as Harden, Murdle, and Murden; "Steerforth" was originally Steerford; "Littimer," the valet, was Lirrimer; "Mr. Dick" first appeared in manuscript as Mr. Robert; while on the draft of title we find the names of "Wellbury," "Flowerbury," "Magbury," and "Topflower," which were never used. The novelist was much startled when Mr. Forster pointed out to him (what he had never previously noticed) that Copperfield's initials were his own reversed, and protested that it was just in keeping with the fates and chances which were always befalling him. "Why else," he said, "should I so obstinately have kept to that name when once it turned up?"

The "Survey" (No. 4) apparently proved the favourite, but it was not adhered to after all, as the words proposed ultimately became these only: "The Personal History, Adventures, Experience, and Observation of David Copperfield the Younger, of Blunderstone Rookery,* which he never meant to be

* The name of Blunderstone was actually taken by Dickens from a direction-post which he saw halfway between Yarmouth and Lowestoft during his visit to the neighbourhood in 1849. He said that he adopted it because he liked the sound of the word.

Published on any Account"; and with this name the story was launched on May 1st, 1849, although in later editions it was curtailed into its simplest form, "David Copperfield."

When meditating the story, Dickens gathered some material for it in the Eastern Counties. It was at one time supposed, from the vividness of David Copperfield's earliest experiences, that the locality must have been familiar to the author's own boyhood, but, when writing to Mr. Forster on January 12th, 1849, he said that he had just visited Yarmouth for the first time,* which town he characterised as "the strangest place in the wide world," and thereupon decided to "try his hand" at it. The outcome of this resolution was that he made it the home of Little Em'ly, and it was on that occasion that the author actually saw the dwelling-house constructed from an old boat, which he has immortalized as the primitive, but cosy, residence of

* In a letter addressed to M. Cerjat, dated December 29th, 1849 (see "The Letters of Charles Dickens," Vol. I., p. 211), the novelist wrote, "I went down into that part of the country" [viz., Norfolk and Suffolk] "on the 7th of January last year," *i.e.* 1848. This must be an oversight, as his letter to Mr. Forster distinctly proves.

Mr. Peggotty. It stood, as described, on the open "Denes" at Yarmouth, between the sea and the town, whence could then be obtained an uninterrupted view of the German Ocean. Protests notwithstanding, this quaint structure was demolished in 1879 or 1880, and a modern villa stands on the site, having inscribed over the door the words "Peggotty's House," in order to preserve the interesting associations of the spot; but from its neat bow windows it is impossible to catch even a glimpse of the sea, so completely is the cottage hemmed in by bricks and mortar.

Although the question of title was satisfactorily disposed of, there were still certain difficulties that beset the novelist at the opening of this romance. "My hand is out in the matter of 'Copperfield,'" he wrote in great tribulation to Mr. Forster. "To-day" [April 19th, 1849] "and yesterday I have done nothing. Though I know what I want to do, I am lumbering on like a stage-waggon, . . . and the long Copperfieldian perspective looks snowy and thick, this fine morning." Once fairly launched, however, the tale bore him irresistibly along; it proceeded rapidly and pleasantly, and more smoothly, perhaps, than any other of his books. On June 6th he said:

"I feel, thank God, quite confident in the story. I have a move in it ready for this month; another for next; and another for the next." On the 25th of the same month he wrote to Mark Lemon, advising him to "Get a clean pocket-handkerchief ready for the close of 'Copperfield' No. 3; 'Simple and quiet, but very natural and touching.'—*Evening Bore.*" (This number contained an affecting account of the death and burial of David's mother.) To the Rev. James White he stated (July 13th, 1850) that he was glad to say "there seems a bright unanimity about 'Copperfield.' I am very much interested in it and pleased with it myself. I have carefully planned out the story, for some time past, to the end, and am making out my purposes with great care." To Sir E. Bulwer Lytton, who admired the novel, he similarly expressed himself, and added: "I have kept and am keeping my mind very steadily upon it." In fact, he was wonderfully in harness; nothing galled or fretted him, and he declared that he felt the story in its minutest point,—a happy mental and physical condition which may be attributed to the fact that at this time he carefully refrained from overtaxing his powers. When preparing the final chapters, however, his pen was exceptionally busy. "I have been tremendously at work these two days," he wrote; "eight hours at a stretch yesterday, and six hours and a half to-day, with the Ham and Steerforth chapter, which has completely knocked me over—utterly defeated me." While the tale was in progress, the author was engaged upon the early numbers of his weekly journal. Writing to Macready on June 11th, 1850, he says: "Between 'Copperfield' and *Household Words*, I am as busy as a bee. May the former be as good a book as I hope it will be for your children's children to read." On October 21st he intimated to his future biographer that the close of the story was at hand: "I am within three pages of the shore," he said; "and am strangely divided, as usual in such cases, between sorrow and joy. Oh, my dear Forster, if I were to say half of what 'Copperfield' makes me feel to-night, how strangely, even to you, I should be turned inside out! I seem to be sending some part of myself into the Shadowy World." Thus we see how real to the great novelist were the plots he invented and the characters he created.

It is now well known that "David Copperfield" is partly an autobiography, although to what extent the world was unaware until the author had passed away. In an unpublished letter addressed by Dickens to Mrs. Howitt, September 7th, 1859, he said that he had worked "many childish experiences and many young struggles into 'Copperfield.'" Its autobiographical facts, however, form only the materials for intellectual and imaginative treatment, and, as Dr. Peter Bayne observes, "it is to the wisdom of that running comment which Dickens makes upon them that they owe their best value." Reading between the lines of this fascinating novel, the nature of the novelist's early misfortunes are revealed to us, such as his uncongenial occupation at the Blacking Warehouse on Hungerford Stairs; we are thus enabled to realise, also, the difficulties he encountered in mastering shorthand, and his anxious attempts at authorship, all of which features in David Copperfield's career correspond with incidents in Charles Dickens's own life, and to this alone may be attributed the principal charm and fascination of the story. Nevertheless, Mr. Forster warns us against assuming too much with respect to the identity of the novelist with his hero, and assures us that "the language of fiction reflects only faintly the narrative of the actual fact." The late Mr. Charles Dickens the Younger, who contended that there is really nothing autobiographical about the book beyond the details already mentioned, has placed on record the following statement :—

"For myself I have only one remark to make as to this matter. In one passage my father says: 'I have never, until I now impart it to this paper, in any burst of confidence with any one, my own wife not excepted, raised the curtain I then dropped, thank God '*; but I have my mother's authority for saying—she told me at the time of the publication of Mr. Forster's first volume, and asked me to make the fact public if, after her death, an opportunity should arise—that the story was eventually read to her in strict confidence by my father, who at the same time intimated his intention of publishing it by-and-bye as a portion of his autobiography. From this purpose she endeavoured to dissuade him: on the ground that he had spoken with undue harshness of his father, and, especially, of his mother: and with so much success that he eventually decided that he would be satisfied with working it into 'David Copperfield,' and would give up the idea of publishing it as it stood. How, after this, the story came to be given to the public I do not know, but I have always thought it a pity that Mr. Forster did not exercise some of that discretion which is always supposed to be left to biographers, but which, unfortunately, they do not always think fit to employ, by omitting

* See the fragment of Dickens's autobiography in Forster's Life of the novelist, Vol. I., Chapters I. and II.

the half-dozen or so lines which cannot but have come as a shock to most people, and the deletion of which would not have affected the interest or value of the story in the slightest degree. That Mr. Forster did not know what had passed between my father and mother as to this matter I think most probable. That he did not take any steps to find out I know to be a fact."

As Charles Dickens's mother unconsciously posed as a model for Mrs. Nickleby, so did his father suggest the personality of Mr. Micawber, in whom are shadowed forth certain peculiarities of action and speech which appertained to Mr. John Dickens. This is current belief, and so much is asserted by Mr. Forster; but the novelist's eldest son has declared it to be absolutely without foundation, "except within the limits of the description given in the autobiographical sketch, and except as to certain odd phrases and turns of expression in speech and letter writing." In support of this, he quotes the following testimony by the novelist: "I know my father to be as kind-hearted and generous a man as ever lived in the world. Everything I can remember of his conduct to his wife, or children, or friends, in sickness or affliction, is beyond all praise. By me as a sick child, he has watched night and day, unwearily and patiently, many nights and days. He never undertook any business, charge, or trust, that he did not zealously, conscientiously, punctually, honourably discharge. His industry has always been untiring." And again: "The longer I live, the better man I think him."

There is, however, a personal sketch in "David Copperfield" which is acknowledged to have been pourtrayed from life, viz., that of the good-natured but eccentric little Miss Mowcher. Her prototype was a neighbour of Dickens, who followed the same occupation as that of the "volatile" lady, and, detecting the portraiture of herself in the novel, she seriously remonstrated with the author for the liberty he had thus taken. On the eve of the tenth number he received from her a vigorous protest, and in writing to Mr. Forster on the subject he said: "It is serio-comic, but there is no doubt one is wrong in being tempted to such a use of power." * He undoubtedly erred in copying too closely the singularity of face and figure, and was shocked at discovering the pain he had unwittingly given. The result was that his intentions as to Miss Mowcher's

* It is interesting to note that in this communication Dickens spells the name "Moucher," instead of "Mowcher," as in the story.

connection with the plot were altered altogether, and to her advantage.

In Mr. Forster's biography there is reference to a "Dora," who met Dickens very early in his career, and who, it has been supposed, inspired the character of David's "child-wife"—a character to whom he became very partial as the story progressed; indeed, a letter from Dickens to his biographer confirms the statement that the Dora in fiction was founded on a Dora in fact, and we are also told that the description of Flora in "Little Dorrit" was derived from the same original.

Dickens's favourite people in "Copperfield" were the Peggotty group, and it is fair to assume that certain characteristics appertaining to Clara Peggotty were derived from Mary Weller, who nursed Charles Dickens when a child. Mr. Forster declares that the portrait of Rosa Dartle was partly drawn from one of the novelist's lady-friends, with whom he was on excellent terms, but whose name is not divulged. Mr. Thomas Traddles, who is finally spoken of in the story as the next Judge, is said to have been intended for Sir T. N. Talfourd, one of the author's oldest friends; their respective initials are practically identical.

"David Copperfield" was published by Messrs. Bradbury and Evans in twenty monthly parts, demy octavo, at one shilling each, having the familiar green pictorial wrappers; the work began in May, 1849, and ended in November, 1850, the last two numbers being issued together in one wrapper. Each part contained two etched illustrations by H. K. Browne; in the first edition the illustrated title-page bears date 1850, which is absent from later editions of the same year. The complete story was published as a guinea volume in November, 1850 (*Collation*—pp. xvi., one unnumbered page of *Errata*, and pp. 624), with a Preface dated "London, October, 1850," and an Inscription to the Hon. Mr. and Mrs. Richard Watson, of Rockingham, Northampton. The work has often been reissued in the same form, green cloth, with or without a date. The first Cheap Edition came in the Second Series (1858), with a new Preface and a frontispiece by H. K. Browne. In the "Charles Dickens" Edition the Preface was considerably altered, and a new paragraph added at the end.

The original MS. and a portion of one of the corrected proofs of "David Copperfield" are at South Kensington. An examination of the manuscript shows that the name of Mr. Dick was originally written Mr. Robert; while in a proof of the fourteenth chapter we find that the allusion to "King Charles the First's head"—about which Mr. Dick was so much concerned—was not contained in the first draft of the story, for the passage then had reference to "the date when that bull got into the china warehouse and did so much mischief." Certain passages were erased from the proof, and some hints and catch-words were set down by the author for the treatment of each chapter, such as the following:—

"First chapter funny. Then go on to Emily. 'Going out with the tide.' Emily to go? No. Yes, and ruined? Next time.* Miss Moucher; impossible. No Steerforth, this time. Keep him out."

The price of a copy of "David Copperfield," in parts as issued, is from £3 to £4. The original Prospectus, headed

* In a letter to M. Cerjat, Dickens wrote (December 29th, 1849): "I hope, in the history of Little Em'ly (who *must* fall—there is no hope for her), to put it before the thoughts of people in a new and pathetic way, and perhaps to do some good." He felt a great hope that he would "be remembered by Little Em'ly a good many years to come."

with the words "The Copperfield Survey of the World as it Rolled" (at first incorporated with the title, but afterwards withdrawn) has been catalogued at £1.

Although rightly considered a *chef d'œuvre*, the circulation of "David Copperfield" was not to be compared with that of previous and succeeding works, the sale of the monthly parts never exceeding 25,000. Mr. Wilkie Collins attributed this decline in the sale to the disappointment created in the public mind by the preceding book, "Dombey and Son." On its completion, however, the story enjoyed an enormous popularity. The author opined that it was appreciated more than any of his other tales, and that he himself preferred it is indicated both in correspondence with friends and in the Preface to later editions, where we read: "Of all my books, I like this the best. It will be easily believed that I am a fond parent of every child of my fancy, and that no one can ever love that family as dearly as I love them. But, like many fond parents, I have in my heart of hearts a favourite child, and his name is 'David Copperfield.'" To Miss Mary Boyle he wrote, "I am not quite sure that I ever did like, or ever shall like, anything quite so well as 'Copperfield'"; and years afterwards, when addressing Mr. Forster, the novelist said: "I read 'David Copperfield' again the other day, and was affected by it to a degree you would hardly believe."

This delightful romance numbered amongst its admirers the most eminent critics of the day. Thackeray's beautiful eulogium, placed in the mouth of one of his characters,* is characteristic of the writer's genial disposition: "How beautiful it is —how charmingly fresh and simple! In those admirable touches of tender humour, a mixture of love and wit—who can equal this great genius?" The night after the Oxford election (1857), in which the author of "Vanity Fair" was an unsuccessful candidate, he gave some readings on behalf of a fund then being raised to the memory of Douglas Jerrold, in the course of which he thus alluded to the writings of Dickens: "I think of these past writers" [Sterne and his "school"], "and of one who lives amongst us now, and am grateful for the innocent laughter, and the sweet and unsullied pages, which the author of 'David Copperfield' gives to my children." It is one of his children, Mrs. Ritchie, herself

* Mr. Brown, in "Sketches and Travels in London," 1856.

an accomplished author, who writes: "I can remember, when 'David Copperfield' came out, hearing him" [her father] "saying with emphasis to my grandmother that 'little Em'ly's letter to old Peggotty was a masterpiece.' I wondered to hear him at the time, for that was not at all the part I cared for most, nor indeed could I imagine how little Em'ly was so stupid as to run away from Peggotty's enchanted house-boat. But we each and all enjoyed in turn our share of those thin green books full of delicious things, and how glad we were when they came to our hands at last, after our elders and our governess and our butler had all read them in turn. . . . The Dickens books were as much part of our home as our own father's." *

The tale was highly extolled by Matthew Arnold, who wrote: "What a pleasure to have the opportunity of praising a work so sound, a work so rich in merits, as 'David Copperfield'! . . . To contemporary work so good as 'David Copperfield' we are in danger of perhaps not paying respect enough, of reading it (for who could help reading it?) too hastily, and then putting it aside for something

* "Chapters from Some Memories," by Anne Thackeray Ritchie, 1894.

else and forgetting it. What treasures of gaiety, invention, life, are in that book! what alertness and resource! what a soul of good-nature and kindness governing the whole!"* The same writer is responsible for the statement that Mr. Gladstone once solaced himself with "David Copperfield" after an illness, "and so set all good Liberals (of whom I wish to be considered one) upon reading it over again." Mr. Ruskin holds the opinion that the storm scene in "David Copperfield" is one of the finest instances of descriptive writing; while Dickens himself thought this particular scene one of the most effective of his public readings. Professor A. W. Ward looks upon the story as "a pearl without a peer among the later fictions of our English school," and as the most perfect, as a work of art, of all Dickens's fictions; while to Dr. Peter Bayne it seemed "to combine the burnished brilliancy of Charlotte Brontë with the ease of Goldsmith."

* *Nineteenth Century*, June, 1881.

"BLEAK HOUSE."

AFTER the publication of "David Copperfield" in volume form a year elapsed before Dickens commenced his next serial story, "Bleak House," the writing of which was begun in his new residence, Tavistock House, Tavistock Square, at the end of November, 1851. He was at first eager to open the novel in that pretty bit of English landscape, Strood Valley, which reminded him always of a Swiss scene; but this was not to be. As in previous instances, he had troubles at the very outset, not the least of which was an intolerable restlessness. "I sit down between whiles," he wrote from Broadstairs, "to think of a new story, and, as it begins to grow, such a torment of a desire to be anywhere but where I am, and to be going I don't know where, I don't know why, takes hold of me, that it is like being *driven away*." However, directly he had settled in Tavistock House he earnestly concentrated his attention upon the tale; and, as generally happened with the more important incidents of his life (but always accidentally), the day was Friday when the first words were penned.

The title of this novel gave rise to considerable discussion, for Dickens invariably found it difficult to satisfy himself in such matters. No less than twelve tentative titles were proposed before that of "Bleak House" was adopted, eight of these indicating that it was originally the author's intention to make a very prominent feature of a certain low neighbourhood which he afterwards so graphically described in the book. The trial titles were :—

1. "Tom-all-Alone's. The Ruined House." 2. "Tom-all-Alone's. The Solitary House that was always shut up." 3. "Bleak House Academy." 4. "The East Wind." 5. "Tom-all-Alone's. The Ruined [House, Building, Factory, Mill] that got into Chancery and never got out." 6. "Tom-all-Alone's. The Solitary House where the Grass grew." 7. "Tom-all-Alone's. The Solitary House that was always shut up and never Lighted." 8. "Tom-all-Alone's. The Ruined House that got into Chancery and never got out." 9. "Tom-all-Alone's. The Solitary House where the Wind howled." 10. "Tom-all-Alone's. The Ruined House that got into Chancery and never got

out." 11. "Bleak House and the East Wind. How they both got into Chancery and never got out." 12. "Bleak House."

In the present work Dickens determined to assail the Court of Chancery by drawing public attention to the enormous waste of time and money which usually characterises its proceedings. He was encouraged in this design by receiving (after two numbers had been written and the first one published) a striking pamphlet, written by Mr. W. Challinor of Leek, containing details relating to this very subject, which were so apposite that the novelist took from them (without change in any material point) the memorable case of Gridley, as related in the fifteenth chapter, this being a suit affecting a single farm valued at not more than £1,200—all that the owner possessed in the world—against which a bill had been filed for a £300 legacy left in the will bequeathing the farm. In reality there was only one defendant, but in the bill, by the rule of the Court, there were seventeen; and, after two years had been occupied over the seventeen answers, everything had to begin over again because an eighteenth had been accidentally omitted, the costs thus incurred amounting to three times the amount of the legacy.

As Mr. Challinor observed, "What a mockery of justice this is!"

Charles Dickens, ever eager to expose public grievances, inserted in his newly-founded periodical, *Household Words*, an article entitled "Martyrs in Chancery," which, owing to certain inaccuracies, brought upon him an antagonist in the person of Sir Edward Sugden (afterwards Lord St. Leonards), who presented a correct version of the affair in the *Times*, January 7th, 1851. The novelist, however, resolved to give even greater publicity to the gross abuse of Chancery practice, and so introduced in "Bleak House" the famous suit of Jarndyce *v.* Jarndyce, based upon the notorious Jennings case, which has been before the Court so many times during the last ninety years, and still continues to haunt those legal purlieus. In this remarkable action the vast estates of Earl Howe are involved; the property in litigation (comprising about one-half of the ground on which Birmingham stands) belonged to William Jennings, who died in 1798, at the age of ninety-seven, and respecting which the decisions of the Court are invariably in favour of the Curzon family, the defendants, who took the earldom in 1821. It is stated that a persevering individual (having interested motives, probably) has for a considerable period been devoting his time and a liberal supply of money in attempting to unravel this strange history, and the very intricate pedigree is said to have been solved at last! *

In consequence of certain statements which reached Dickens respecting the Jarndyce case, the novelist was impelled to defend his assertions. In his Preface he declared that everything set forth in the pages of "Bleak House" concerning the Court of Chancery is "substantially true, and within the truth," and further intimated that if he wanted other author-

* On October 25th, 1895, a motion in connection with this suit was brought before Mr. Justice Kekewich (Earl Howe *v.* Willis), during the hearing of which it appeared that the defendant had lately been serving notices on some of the plaintiff's tenants in Suffolk, not to pay their rents to Earl Howe, who thereupon brought an action to restrain Willis from interfering with his possession of the estate. The surname of the opposing litigants is sometimes given as Jennens, and it seems that the testator (an old miser who lived at Acton, in Suffolk) made a will, but neither it nor executors could be found. Eventually the heir-at-law was traced in the person of the great-great-grandson of C. Jennings of Gopsal, the eldest uncle of the deceased, who then entered into possession of the property.

ities for "Jarndyce and Jarndyce," he "could rain them on these pages, to the shame of—a parsimonious public." Similarly, the extraordinary death of Krook by spontaneous combustion (as related in the novel) excited much controversy, that eminent scientist and critic, Mr. George Henry Lewes, being strongly opposed to the validity of the theory admitted by Dickens. The novelist, however, maintained his ground, and cited some notable instances of death thus effected, making especial reference to that of the Countess Cornelia de Bandi Cesenate, which had apparently borne the test of minute investigation. A writer in the *Westminster Review* (October, 1864) refused to accept such evidence as conclusive, and averred that Dickens entirely misconceived the point in issue, the dispute being "not as to the facts, but as to their explanation." It is, perhaps, more to the purpose to remark (as Mr. Percy Fitzgerald reasonably argues) that phenomena so rare become improbable and incongruous in fiction.

Charles Dickens was at work on "Bleak House" all through 1852. In March, when the first number appeared, he was greatly harassed by a disturbed mental condition, and could not make satisfactory progress with the story. Writing to Mr. Forster, he said: "Wild ideas are upon me of going to Paris—Rouen—Switzerland—somewhere—and writing the remaining two-thirds of the next No. aloft in some queer inn room. I have been hanging over it, and have got restless. Want a change I think." This was probably the beginning of an illness (a severe inflammatory pain in the side) to which he subsequently alluded in a letter of sympathy to Mr. Wilkie Collins—an illness which caused him much suffering of another kind, "the fear of not being able to come up to time." The inability to "grind sparks out of his dull blade" (as he characterised his work at "Bleak House") continuing to worry him, he thought of going to Switzerland—a scheme which ended in a flight to Dover, where he was at last able to settle down at his desk. In July matters looked more promising, as we read in a letter of that date, addressed to Miss Mary Boyle: "I foresee, I think, some very good things in 'Bleak House.' . . . I behold them in the months ahead and weep."

Early in 1853 the excessive strain of attempting too much began to tell upon him. "Hypochondriacal whisperings tell me that I am rather overworked," he complained to Mr. Forster. On June 13th he was again in Boulogne, thankful for escaping a breakdown in his writing, *à propos* of which he said: "If I had substituted anybody's knowledge of myself for my own, and lingered in London, I never could have got through." It was during his stay at this French watering-place, in August of the same year, that he finished the story, which, as we have seen, did not flow from his pen with as much ease and fluency as usual.

"Bleak House" was issued by Messrs. Bradbury and Evans in twenty monthly parts, demy octavo, green wrappers, at one shilling each, commencing in March, 1852, and ending in September, 1853, Parts 19 and 20 forming a double number. The work contained forty etched illustrations by H. K. Browne, and was dedicated, "as a Remembrance of our Friendly Union, to my Companions in the Guild of Literature and Art." * The complete story was published in September, 1853, in one volume, cloth, at a guinea—*Collation*, pp. xvi., 624. It has often been reissued in

* This Guild, founded in 1851, by Dickens and Lord Lytton, was intended for the benefit of those authors and artists who, through misfortune, were unable to help themselves. Unhappily, the scheme proved abortive.

the same form, with or without a date, the first Cheap Edition, with a frontispiece by H. K. Browne, appearing in the Second Series (Messrs. Bradbury and Evans, 1858), cloth, at five shillings.

The original MS. and the corrected proofs of "Bleak House" are at South Kensington. A copy of the first edition in parts, as issued, is valued at £2, and in cloth at from £1 to £2.

The sale of "Bleak House" during its publication in numbers proved eminently satisfactory. In March it reached 30,000, and subsequently increased to nearly 40,000, the circulation in November being half as large again as that of "David Copperfield"—indeed, there can be no doubt that the popularity of the latter work considerably enhanced the demand for its successor. According to the author's testimony, "Bleak House" took extraordinarily, especially during the last five or six months of its issue, and "retained its immense circulation from the first, beating dear old 'Copperfield' by a round ten thousand or more."

As previously stated, Dickens's first intention was to have made Poor Jo, the crossing-sweeper, and his repulsive environment more prominent in the story; this is indicated by the fact that its earliest title was taken from those tumbling tenements in Chancery, "Tom-all-Alone's," around which so much of the touching pathos of the story moves. The graphic picture of that poverty-stricken locality is said to have been suggested by a similar rookery in the neighbourhood of the Convict Prison at Chatham, which must have been familiar to Dickens in his boyhood. With respect to the origin of the name, "Tom-all-Alone's," Mr. Hobbes, the cashier of Chatham Dockyard, informed Mr. Langton that about 1747 one Thomas Clark, of Old Brompton, bought a piece of waste ground outside the town, and built himself a house there, where he resided quite alone for twenty-five years; when returning home of an evening he used to cry, "Tom's all alone!"—hence the curious nomenclature of the spot. Clark eventually married, and his descendants formed quite a distinct colony, living here until the Prison authorities acquired the land.

Poor Jo is generally considered to be, without doubt, one of the most impressive instances of character-painting in the book. An American critic remarks:—

"We read the death of a good many eminent men without an emotion; . . . but we cannot withhold a tear when we read the death of poor

Jo, and when he is 'moved on' for the last time we too are moved. Yet we know all the time that poor Jo is an unreal phantom—a mere shadowy outline, raised by a few strokes of a steel pen; yet we weep over him and give him the sympathies which we withhold from the real Jo's we encounter in our daily walks."

Concerning this story, Dean Ramsay wrote to Mr. Forster:—

"We have been reading 'Bleak House' 'aloud.' Surely it is one of the most powerful and successful! What a triumph is Jo! Uncultured nature is *there* indeed; the intimations of true heart-feeling, the glimmerings of higher feeling, all are there; but everything still consistent and in harmony. . . . To my mind, nothing in the field of fiction is to be found in English literature surpassing the death of Jo!"

When Miss Jennie Lee (Mrs. Burnett) impersonated the character of "Jo" in Edinburgh, the late Professor Blackie called upon the clergy of all denominations "to go to the Theatre Royal to learn a lesson on the duty of man to his fellows, and to witness a performance as powerful for good as the grandest sermon ever preached."

The burial-ground (long disused) of St. Mary-le-Strand is believed by many to be the particular God's-acre associated by Dickens with the story. At the end of a tunnel-like passage leading from Russell

Court, Drury Lane, may still be seen a gate with iron bars which, in some respects, is identical with that through which Jo pointed out to Lady Dedlock the last resting-place of "Nemo," his only benefactor.* In 1883, public interest was excited in this out-of-the-way graveyard, owing to the fact that, under the auspices of the Metropolitan Gardens Association, it was transformed into a recreation ground by the removal of gravestones to the boundary wall and the place asphalted over, while a drinking-fountain has been erected on the playground in memory of the great novelist. According to local tradition, Dickens's scathing exposure of this burial-ground caused it to be the very first place in London to be closed by official authority as an improper place of intramural sepulture; and, to some extent, this is corroborated by Mr. Forster, who states that Dickens was greatly interested in the movement for closing town and city graveyards (see the close of the eleventh chapter of "Bleak House"), and providing places of burial under State supervision. It is believed by some that Dickens obtained the material for his dramatic picture from

* Recent demolitions have swept away nearly the whole of Russell Court, but the gate yet remains *in situ*.

a similar graveyard in Bream's Buildings (Fetter Lane end), although the character of the place has been changed out of all recognition. It is still an enclosed space, the gravestones that remain (some of which bear seventeenth-century dates) being placed in a row against the Board School building on the north side.

There is a common supposition that "Bleak House" at Broadstairs ("Fort House" being its true designation) is the original of that which gives its name to the story, while local tradition asserts that the greater part of Dickens's novel was written there. This, however, is incorrect, and we are justified in looking for Bleak House where the novelist himself placed it, viz., near St. Albans. It is interesting to mention that, in 1872, "Phiz" rented a house then bordering on the fields in Ladbroke Grove Road, Notting Hill, which, from its exposed position, and in remembrance probably of one of his greatest triumphs as an illustrator, he named "Bleak House." Respecting the identity of Chesney Wold we have more tangible evidence, as Dickens himself says, in a letter to the Hon. Mrs. Watson, of Rockingham Castle: "In some of the descriptions of Chesney Wold, I have taken many bits, chiefly about trees and shadows, from observations made at Rockingham. I wonder whether you have ever thought so!"

"Bleak House" is not merely stored with familiar localities, but includes a number of portraits. Two of these presentments found prototypes in well-known *littérateurs*—W. S. Landor and Leigh Hunt—who were personal friends of the novelist. Landor is acknowledged to be the original of Lawrence Boythorne, and it seems that it was one of his whimsical bursts of comical extravagance on the subject of Little Nell, in "The Old Curiosity Shop" (his favourite character in prose fiction), which suggested to Dickens the idea of representing him as the boisterous Boythorne, the likeness being generally recognised at the time. Mrs. Lynn Linton, who first met the novelist at Landor's house in Bath, once asked the "dear old man" if he had ever read "Bleak House," and the answer came, short and sharp, "No, and never shall"—thus proving that he himself identified the portrait. That Landor did not seriously resent the liberty thus taken with his personality is proved by the fact that his "Imaginary Conversations of Greeks and Romans," published during the time "Bleak House" was being issued, contains a most friendly Dedication to Charles Dickens. It is also recorded by Mr. J. T. Fields that, when he once talked the matter over with Dickens, the latter said, "Landor always took that presentation of himself in hearty good-humour, and seemed rather proud of the picture."*

On the other hand, the delineation of Leigh Hunt as Harold Skimpole occasioned much offence and involved an awkward interpretation. When the friends of the essayist protested against so unfavourable a presentment of the author of "Rimini," Dickens's defence was that the manner and not the character was borrowed. Leigh Hunt's eldest son, Mr. Thornton Hunt, referring to certain qualities of head and heart that appertained to his father, spoke of "his animation, his sympathy with what was gay and pleasurable, his avowed doctrine of cultivating cheerfulness," traits "on which he himself insisted *with a sort of gay and ostenta-*

* "Yesterdays with Authors," by J. T. Fields, 1872. Landor, who was godfather to Dickens's second son, was pronounced by Mr. Forster to be "a man, genial, joyous, kind; and of a nature large and generous to excess; but of a temper uncontrollably impetuous, and prone to act from undisciplined impulse. . . . He was apt gradually to become tyrannical where he had power, and rebellious where he had not."

tious wilfulness"; he also alluded to his father's incapacity to understand figures, all of which peculiarities, in an exaggerated form, are undoubtedly reminiscent of Skimpole.* When, after Leigh Hunt's decease, the subject was revived in American journals, Dickens thus endeavoured to explain matters in an article entitled "Leigh Hunt: a Remonstrance":—

"The fact is this: Exactly those graces and charms of manner which are remembered in the words we have quoted were remembered by the author of the work of fiction in question when he drew the character in question. Above all other things, that 'sort of gay and ostentatious wilfulness' in the humouring of a subject, which had many times delighted him, and impressed him as being unspeakably whimsical and attractive, was the airy quality he wanted for the man he invented. Partly for this reason, and partly (he has since often grieved to think) for the pleasure it afforded him to find that delightful manner reproducing itself under his hand, he yielded to the temptation of too often making the character *speak* like his old friend. He no more thought, God forgive him! that the admired original would ever be charged with the imaginary vices of the fictitious creature than he has himself ever thought of charging the blood of Desdemona and Othello on the innocent Academy model who sat for Iago's leg in the picture. Even as to the mere occasional manner,

---

* *Vide* Introduction prefixed to the new edition of Leigh Hunt's Autobiography.

he meant to be so cautious and conscientious that he privately referred the two proof-sheets of the first number of that book to two intimate literary friends of Leigh Hunt [Procter and Forster], and altered the whole of that part of the text on their discovering too strong a resemblance to his 'way.'"*

This controversial theme was again renewed directly after Dickens's death,† when Mr. Edmund Ollier, an old friend of Leigh Hunt, pointed out that not only did the novelist himself correct the misapprehension in 1859, but that, during Hunt's life and after the publication of "Bleak House," he wrote a most genial paper about him in *Household Words*.‡ Mr. Ollier also affirmed that Dickens expressed to Leigh Hunt personally his regret at the Skimpole mistake.§ Concerning this subject Mr. Forster writes :—

"Though a want of consideration was thus shown to the friend whom the character would be likely to recall to many readers, it is nevertheless very certain that the intention of Dickens was not at first, or at any time, an unkind one. He erred from thoughtlessness only. . . . Perhaps the only person acquainted with the

---

* *All the Year Round*, December 24th, 1859.

† *Daily News*, June 10th, 1870.

‡ "By Rail to Parnassus." *Household Words*, June 16th, 1855.

§ *Daily News*, June 11th, 1870.

original who failed to recognise the copy, was the original himself (a common case); but good-natured friends in time told Hunt everything, and painful explanations followed."

Referring to the Leigh Hunt incident, Mr. Wilkie Collins wrote in his privately-marked copy of Mr. Forster's biography of the novelist: "At Dickens's own house, when Leigh Hunt was one of his guests at dinner on that occasion, Hunt directly charged Dickens with taking the character of Harold Skimpole from the character of Leigh Hunt, and protested strongly. I was not present, but Dickens told me what had happened."

The "Bleak House" novel brought down upon the author's head severe denunciations in certain quarters. The late Lord Denman, Lord Chief Justice of England, who was an enthusiastic promoter of the anti-slavery movement, strongly objected (in letters contributed by him to the *Standard* during the publication of "Bleak House") to Dickens's satirical allusions to Borrioboola Gha: "We do not say," wrote his lordship, "that he actually defends slavery or the slave-trade; but he takes pains to discourage, by ridicule, the effort now making to put them down," and thus does his best "to replunge the world into bar-

barism." Sir Joseph Arnould, the author of a "Memoir of Thomas, First Lord Denman" (1873), rightly contends that such strictures were unjustifiable, and some members of his lordship's family became anxious to excuse as far as possible, on the ground of morbid excitement and over-wrought feeling, this unfortunate indulgence in "letter-writing"; but Dickens informed them that he had "cleared his mind" of Lord Denman's accusations, adding, "I know I deserve his former and wiser judgment, and I cancel the rest for ever." Lord Denman likewise angrily declared the "disgusting picture" of Mrs. Jellaby to be a "laboured work of art"; that if it were a real likeness it was hardly worth the taking, but if meant to represent a class, no representation was ever more false. The novelist's somewhat extravagant rendering of the Borrioboola Gha picture was also boldly attacked by Miss Harriet Martineau, who, by the way, is assumed to have been the original of Mrs. Jellaby.

It is worthy of record that, during a discussion in the *Daily Chronicle* on the subject of boys' literature, a correspondent whose letter bore the signature "Ex-Arab" declared that he became a city wastrel at the age of eleven, and referred to certain ragged copies of boys' publications, the reading of which he and his fellow-arabs enjoyed. In some fragmentary form they possessed those chapters of "Bleak House" relating to Jo, and the author of the letter in question asks, "Have any of us ever read anything since that gave us such pleasure as Jo's story did? I think not. As far as I am concerned, my answer is emphatic,—nothing." Such an unexpected tribute as this, from one whose early days were spent much in the same manner as Poor Jo's, would have afforded the novelist much gratification.

A very interesting pamphlet was published by H. Elliott in 1856, some time after the appearance of the novel. It was entitled "Bleak House: a Narrative of Real Life; being a faithful detail of facts connected with a suit in the Irish Court of Chancery, from the year 1826 to 1851. Showing what a lawsuit really is, apart from any circumstance of fiction or romance." That it was Dickens's story, however, which proved the more efficacious in drawing attention to a real public grievance, and in bringing about certain reforms, is a fact not likely to be controverted.

"LITTLE DORRIT."

MR. FORSTER states that "Little Dorrit" took its origin from the notion Dickens had of a leading man for a story who should bring about all the mischief in it, lay it all on Providence, and say at every fresh calamity, "Well, it's a mercy, however, nobody was to blame you know!" This idea was evidently abandoned as the story developed. In January, 1855 (that is, six months before "Little Dorrit" was written), the novelist began a book of memoranda for possible use in his work. In it he jotted down in a haphazard manner any hints or suggestions that occurred to him—such as a mere piece of imagery, the outline of a subject or character, a bit of description or dialogue; and here we may find some fancies for "Little Dorrit." For example, the home of the Barnacle family is thus noted:—

"Our House. Whatever it is, it is in a first-rate situation, and a fashionable neighbourhood.

(Auctioneer called it 'a gentlemanly residence.') A series of little closets squeezed up into the corner of a dark street—but a Duke's Mansion round the corner. The whole house just large enough to hold a vile smell. The air breathed in it, at the best of times, a kind of Distillation of Mews."

Again, there was an entry made of the author's original conception of the close of old Dorrit's life:—

"First sign of the father failing and breaking down. Cancels long interval. Begins to talk about the turnkey who first called him the Father of the Marshalsea—as if he were still living. 'Tell Bob I want to speak to him. See if he is on the Lock, my dear.'"

Here is the first notion of Clennam's reverse of fortune :—

"His falling into difficulty, and himself imprisoned in the Marshalsea. Then she, out of all her wealth and changed station, comes back in her old dress, and devotes herself in the old way."

"He seems," says Mr. Forster, "to have designed, for the sketches of Society in the same tale, a 'full-length portrait of his lordship, surrounded by worshippers'; of which, beside that brief memorandum, only his first draft of the general outline was worked at" :—

"Sensible men enough, agreeable men enough,

independent men enough in a certain way;—but the moment they begin to circle round my lord, and to shine with a borrowed light from his lordship, heaven and earth how mean and subservient! What a competition and outbidding of each other in servility!"

In the same note-book we find that what he originally meant to express by Mrs. Clennam has narrower limits, and a character less repellent, than it assumed in the story:—

"Bed-ridden (or room-ridden) twenty—five-and-twenty—years; any length of time. As to most things, kept at a standstill all the while Thinking of altered streets as the old streets—changed things as the unchanged things—the youth or girl I quarrelled with all those years ago, as the same youth or girl now. Brought out of doors by an unexpected exercise of my latent strength of character, and then how strange!"

The following memorandum presents a picture which seems to live with a more touching effect in his first pleasing fancy of it, viz., the description of the river and ferryman in the sixteenth chapter:—

"The ferryman on a peaceful river, who has been there from youth, who lives, who grows old, who does well, who does ill, who changes, who dies—the river runs six hours up and six hours down, the current sets off that point, the same allowance must be made for the drifting of the boat, the same tune is always played by the rippling water against the prow."

The final note reads thus: "The unwieldy ship taken in tow by the snorting little steam tug," here being prefigured the patriarch Casby and his agent Panks. Dickens's biographer states that the novelist prided himself on the creation of Henry Gowan, as being something forcible and novel. He also had in Miss Wade what he believed to be a new idea, that of "making the introduced story (Chapter XXI.) so fit into surroundings impossible of separation from the main story, as to make the blood of the book circulate through both"; but in this he apparently did not succeed.

The first title chosen for the tale was entirely different from that eventually adopted. In a letter to the Hon. Mrs. Watson (dated September 16th, 1855) he wrote: "Catherine [Mrs. Dickens] tells me that you want to know the name of my new book. I cannot bear that you should know it from any one but me. It will not be made public until the end of October; the title is

'NOBODY'S FAULT.'

Keep it as the apple of your eye—an expressive form of speech, though I have not the least idea of what it means."

Four numbers had been written, of which the first was on the eve of publication, before this title was changed.

Dickens began the writing of "Little Dorrit" at Tavistock House in May, 1855, and, as usual, found it difficult to make a good start. In a letter to Mr. Wilkie Collins at this time he said: "The restless condition in which I wander up and down my room with the first page of my new book before me defies all description. I feel as if nothing would do but setting up in a Balloon. It might be inflated in the garden in front, but I am afraid of its scarcely clearing those little houses." Presently we find the novelist excusing himself from an engagement because "the story is breaking out all round me, and I am going off down the railroad to humour it." When he reached the second number he expressed dissatisfaction, and notified that he had half a mind to begin again, and afterwards work in what he had done; for the thought occurred to him that he had missed an effect. "It struck me," he wrote, "that it would be a new thing to show people coming together, in a chance way, as fellow-travellers, and being in the same place, ignorant of one another, as happens in life; and to connect them afterwards, and to make the waiting for that connection a part of the interest." The change was not made, however; and Mr. Forster inferred from the mention of it, as well as from other intimations, that "the old, unstinted, irrepressible flow of fancy had received temporary check." Indeed, the novelist's hesitancy is indicated in the plan prepared for the first number, the production of which occasioned much trouble and labour.* In August he wrote: "I am just now getting to work on number three: sometimes enthusiastic, more often dull enough. There is an enormous outlay in the Father of the Marshalsea chapter, in the way of getting a great lot of matter into a small space. I am not quite resolved, but I have a great idea of overwhelming that family with wealth. Their condition would be very curious. I can make Dorrit very strong in the story, I hope."

In writing "Little Dorrit" the author determined to denounce in vigorous terms the dilatory system of conducting public business as adopted by Government officials—a system which, in a spirit of ridicule, he designated by the word "Circumlocution." "The mere name of the Circumlocution Office," says Professor

* See *facsimile*, Forster's "Life of Charles Dickens," Vol. III., 134.

Ward, "was a stroke of genius, one of those phrases of Dickens which Professor Masson justly describes as, whether exaggerated or not, 'efficacious for social reform.'" It is a remarkable fact that, soon after the story was published, Dickens's friend and brother-novelist, Lord Lytton (when a Minister), unwittingly furnished a specimen of the manner in which public business was despatched. Receiving an important deputation at the Colonial Office, he explained (as the reason for his ignorance, until that moment, of the matter under discussion) that "papers of importance passed through several departments, and required time for inspection; first, they were sent to the Emigration Board, then to *another* office, and then to the Secretary of State, who might refer it to some other department." Query, what other department? This is what Mr. Clennam always "wanted to know." In January, 1856, the number containing the literary lashing of "Circumlocution" was published, *à propos* of which Dickens wrote: "I have a grim pleasure upon me to-night in thinking that the Circumlocution Office sees the light, and in wondering what effect it will make." The Circumlocution heroes led to the Society scenes, the Hampton

Court dowager-sketches, and Mr. Gowan; all parts of one satire levelled against prevailing political and social vices. Dickens had now obtained a thorough grip of his story. "My head" [he wrote from Paris on January 30th, 1856] "really stings with the visions of the book, and I am going, as the French say, to disembarrass it by plunging out into some of the strange places I glide into of nights in these latitudes."

Throughout the year 1856 the publication of "Little Dorrit" was proceeding in regular monthly instalments. In a letter addressed to Mr. Wilkie Collins in April, Dickens remarked: "The first blank page of 'Little Dorrit,' No. 8, now eyes me on this desk with a pressing curiosity. It will get nothing out of me to-day, I distinctly perceive." In October he informed the Hon. Mrs. Watson that he wrote the first chapter of Book the Second for her, adding "and I hoped in writing it, that you would think so. All those remembrances are fresh in my mind, as they often are, and gave me an extraordinary interest in recalling the past. I should have been grievously disappointed if you had not been pleased, for I took aim at you with a most determined intention." The chapter referred to treats of the visit of the Dorrit family to the Great St. Bernard—an expedition which he made himself, in company with Mr. and Mrs. Watson and other friends. The winter of 1856 found him not only engaged upon the story, but immersed in the excitement of private theatricals at Tavistock House, whence he addresses Miss Marguerite Power (December 15th): "Your friend has been writing 'Little Dorrit,' etc., etc., in corners, like the Sultan's groom, who was turned upside down by the Genie"—thus alluding to the "terrific preparations" for acting "Twelfth Night," the various rooms in his domicile being temporarily monopolised by painters, gas-fitters, dress-makers, etc. In a letter to Macready two days previously he thus describes the situation: "Calm amidst the wreck" [of the premises, occasioned by the above-mentioned disturbance of his domestic environment], "your aged friend glides away on the 'Dorrit' stream, forgetting the uproar for a stretch of hours, refreshes himself with a ten or twelve miles walk, puts his head foremost into foaming rehearsals, placidly emerges for editorial purposes, smokes over buckets of distemper with Mr. Stanfield, again calmly floats upon the 'Dorrit' waters."

It was while busy with "Little Dorrit"

that Dickens acquired the old-fashioned house in which he had so long desired to reside—Gad's Hill Place. Here, in May, 1857, he completed the story, intimating the fact in the following jubilant note to Mr. Wilkie Collins: "Thank God, I *have* finished. On Sunday last I wrote the two little words of three letters each."

In "Little Dorrit" a prominent place is given to that notorious debtors' prison, the Marshalsea. Of this establishment Dickens ever retained painful recollections, for here, early in the 'twenties, his father was for a time incarcerated, and here, when ten years old, the future novelist visited his unfortunate parent, accompanying him to his room "on the top story but one," where the poor boy "cried very much." These early reminiscences of the Marshalsea were subsequently utilised by Dickens while writing some of his stories: mention is made of the gaol in "Pickwick" as the place where George Heyling was detained in custody; in "David Copperfield," where doubtless the associations were remembered in connection with another debtors' prison, viz., the King's Bench, the scene of Mr. Micawber's trials; but especially in "Little Dorrit," where so much of the plot of that romance relates to the life of the Dorrit family within the grim walls of the Marshalsea. In the novel now under consideration Dickens entirely relied upon a marvellous memory for his vivid description of the prison, as in the Preface he tells us it was not until the completion of the tale that he decided to revisit the old spot for the purpose of ascertaining whether any part of the building was then standing. Although the gloomy structure had undergone considerable change, he identified a part of it in which were preserved the rooms that arose in his mind's eye when he became Little Dorrit's biographer, and pointed out to a lad whom he met there (" the smallest boy I ever conversed with, carrying the largest baby I ever saw ") the window of the room where Little Dorrit was born, and where her father lived so long. Writing to Mr. Forster at this time, he says : " There is a room there—still standing, to my amazement—that I think of taking ! It is the room through which the ever-memorable signers of Captain Porter's petition filed off in my boyhood. The spikes are gone, and the wall is lowered, and anybody can go out now who likes to go, and is not bedridden. . . ." The paving-stones which the novelist states to be then existing have long disappeared; indeed, since his death that portion of the Borough has been transformed, although the title of the Marshalsea is preserved in the name of one of the new streets, while to various portions of a surviving wall of the gaol are attached some large enamelled tablets, announcing that this is "the site of the old Marshalsea Prison, made famous by Charles Dickens in his well-known 'Little Dorrit.'" There is also, by the way, a Dorrit Street, which similarly perpetuates the associations of the locality. The prison itself was pulled down in 1887; shortly before it disappeared visitors to the building recognised its various features from Dickens's description, thus testifying to its accuracy.

That nest of tenements near Ely Place, Holborn, called "Bleeding Heart Yard," so graphically pictured in "Little Dorrit" as the home of the Plornish family, has also been demolished within recent years. The scene of dilapidated desolation which it presented at the time of its destruction is well pourtrayed in *Chambers's Journal*, October 9th, 1886, where the writer surmises that "visitors will probably soon have some difficulty in finding out even its site."

We learn that the portrait of Flora in "Little Dorrit" was derived from the same living original as the Dora of "David

Copperfield," although it finds an entirely different development in the later story. Dickens, besides highly enjoying his conception of Mr. F's Aunt, was very partial to Flora and her surroundings. "There are some things in Flora in number seven," he wrote, "that seem to me to be extraordinarily droll, with something serious at the bottom of them after all. . . . Nothing in Flora made me laugh so much as the confusion of ideas between gout flying upwards, and its soaring with Mr. F—— to another sphere." Mr. Forster used jocularly to tell Dickens he had no belief in any but the fictitious Dora, until the incident of a sudden reappearance of the real one in his life, nearly six years after "Copperfield" was written, convinced him there had been a more actual foundation for those chapters in his book than his biographer previously imagined. *À propos* of the reality of the association, it is interesting to quote the following from a letter written by the novelist to the late Duke of Devonshire: "I am so glad you like Flora. It came into my head one day that we have all had our Floras, and that it was a half-serious, half-ridiculous truth which had never been told. It is a wonderful gratification to me to find that everybody knows her. Indeed, some people seem to think I have done them a personal injury, and that their individual Floras (God knows where they are, or who!) are each and all Little Dorrits."

Another character in the tale, Mr. Merdle, was admitted by the author to be a drawing of John Sadleir, an Irish banker. Concerning this creation Dickens wrote in the Preface: "If I might make so bold as to defend that extravagant conception, Mr. Merdle, I would hint that it originated after the Railroad-share epoch, in the times of a certain Irish bank, and of one or two other equally laudable enterprises." He informed Mr. Forster with even greater distinctness that, although he had the general idea of the Society business before the Sadleir affair, he "shaped Mr. Merdle himself out of that precious rascality." *

"Little Dorrit" was issued by Messrs. Bradbury and Evans in twenty monthly

* Mr. Percy Fitzgerald points out that there is a slight confusion here, as the Railroad-share epoch was long before the days of the Tipperary bank with which Sadleir was connected. John Sadleir committed suicide, the act of self-destruction taking place in the descending ground just behind Dickens's favourite "Jack Straw's Castle," on Hampstead Heath.

parts, green wrappers, at one shilling each, commencing in December, 1855, and ending in June, 1857—Parts 19 and 20 forming a double number. The work contained forty etched illustrations by H. K. Browne, and a Dedication to Clarkson Stanfield, R.A. The complete story was published in June in one volume, cloth, at one guinea—*Collation*, pp. xiv., 625. It has often been reissued in the same form, with or without a date. The first Cheap Edition was fourth of the Second Series (1861), and contained a frontispiece by Marcus Stone, R.A.

The present price of a very fine copy of "Little Dorrit," in parts as issued, is from £2 10*s*. to £3 10*s*.; if bound, about £1. Part 16 should contain a slip on which is printed the following explanation: "By an oversight of the Author's, which he did not observe until it was too late for correction in the first impression of the Number for last month (xv.), the name RIGAUD is used in the seventeenth chapter of the Second Book, instead of BLANDOIS. The personage in the story who assumed the latter name, is habitually known to the Author by the former, as his real one; and hence the mistake. It is set right, if the reader will have the goodness to substitute the word BLANDOIS for RIGAUD, in that chapter when it occurs. The chapter commences at page 467, and ends at page 474." The original MS. and corrected proofs of the story are at South Kensington.

The sale of "Little Dorrit" began exceedingly well. Of the first Part (published at Christmas, 1855) at least 40,000 copies were sold, and Dickens wrote exultingly: "'Little Dorrit' has beaten even 'Bleak House' out of the field. It is a most tremendous start, and I am overjoyed at it." Of the second Part no less than 35,000 were disposed of on New Year's Day, 1856; indeed, the public showed no falling-off in its enormous numbers. As might be expected, the minds of the critics were speedily exercised as to the merits and demerits of the story. That Dickens was anxious to avoid any mental disquietude that might be occasioned by reading adverse criticisms is indicated in a letter to Mr. Forster at this time: "I was ludicrously foiled here the other night in a resolution I have kept for twenty years not to know of any attack upon myself, by stumbling, before I could pick myself up, on a short extract in the *Globe* from *Blackwood's Magazine*, informing me that 'Little Dorrit' is 'Twaddle.' I was sufficiently put out by it to be angry with myself for being such a fool, and then pleased with myself for having so long been constant to a good resolution."

In July, 1857, the *Edinburgh Review* published a caustic article entitled "The License of Modern Novelists," the writer accusing Dickens of selecting "one or two popular cries of the day, to serve as seasoning to the dish which he sets before his readers," and reproaching him for his "unjust" and "cruel" imputations against the Government, the judges, and private individuals. This discerning critic suggested that the catastrophe in the thirty-first chapter of "Little Dorrit" was "evidently borrowed from the recent fall of houses in Tottenham Court Road" [Messrs. Maple's], "which happens to have appeared in the newspapers at a convenient moment." The novelist replied to this not very skilful diatribe in a short and spirited rejoinder in *Household Words* (August 1st, 1857), entitled "Curious Misprint in the *Edinburgh Review*," where he succeeded in refuting this and similar misstatements, at the same time pointing out that, so far as the fall of houses in Tottenham Court Road was concerned, it will be seen that the disaster referred to in the tale was "carefully prepared for from the very first presentation of the old house in the story, . . . that the catastrophe was written, was engraven on steel, was printed, had passed through the hands of compositors, readers for the press, and pressmen, and was in type and in proof . . . before the accident in Tottenham Court Road occurred." With reference to the title bestowed by Dickens upon his defence, it should be explained that his critic, complaining of the novelist's attack upon the Government, had cited the case of Mr. Rowland Hill, asking whether the Circumlocution Office neglected, traduced, and ruined *him*? The reference caused Dickens to say that "the curious misprint here is the name of Mr. Rowland Hill," whom he declared the Government *had* treated in the manner of the "Circumlocution Office," and if he had not been "in toughness a man of a hundred thousand . . . the Circumlocution Office would have made a dead man of him long and long ago." The novelist concludes his trenchant reply with a hint that the *Edinburgh Review* should "take its next opportunity of manfully expressing its regret that in too distempered a zeal for the Circumlocution Office, it has been betrayed, as to that Tottenham Court Road assertion, into a hasty substitution of untruth for truth." In the succeeding number of the *Review* there accordingly appeared the following semi-apologetic "Note on His Answer":—

> "In answer to some of the remarks contained in our review of 'Little Dorrit,' Mr. Dickens states, in the *Household Words* of the 1st of August, that the catastrophe of that tale formed part of the original plan, and was not suggested by a contemporary occurrence. The coincidence we pointed out was therefore accidental."

There is, however, no reference here to the Rowland Hill "misprint"!

Mr. Forster believed that, on the whole, "Little Dorrit" made no material addition to Dickens's reputation. "The defect in the book," he thought, "was less the absence of excellent character or keen observation, than the want of ease and coherence among the figures of the story, and of a central interest in the plan of it." Concerning the Dorrits he remarks: "The Marshalsea part of the tale undoubtedly was excellent, and there was masterly treatment of character in the contrasts of the brothers Dorrit; but of the family generally it may be said that its least important members had most of his genius in them."

Professor Ward, who admires the

Circumlocution Office passages, considers that Dickens was not at his best when he wrote "Little Dorrit." This, too, was doubtless Thackeray's opinion, judging by an anecdote recorded by the late Mr. Edmund Yates. "Once," he remarks, "when I was speaking of the ruthless strictures of the *Saturday Review* on 'Little Dorrit,' Thackeray, agreeing with me in the main, added, with that strange, half-humorous, half-serious look, 'though, between ourselves, my dear Yates, "Little Dorrit" is Dead Stupid.'"

About four months after Dickens's death, an incident happened that would have more than counteracted the effects upon the author's mind of the most unfavourable comments upon "Little Dorrit." The scene was the meeting of Bismarck and Jules Favre under the walls of Paris; as the Prussian was waiting to open fire on the city, the Frenchman was engaged in the arduous task of showing the wisdom of not doing it, and "while the two eminent statesmen were trying to find a basis of negotiation, Von Moltke was seated in a corner reading 'Little Dorrit.'" One is inclined to ask, with Mr. Forster, "Who will doubt that the chapter on 'How Not to do it' was then absorbing the old soldier's attention?"

"A TALE OF TWO CITIES."

TOWARDS the close of January, 1858, Dickens wrote to Mr. Forster: "Growing inclinations of a fitful and undefined sort are upon me sometimes to fall to work on a new book. Then I think I had better not worry my worried mind yet awhile. Then I think it would be of no use if I did, for I couldn't settle to one occupation.—And that's all!" Again, three days later: "If I can discipline my thoughts into the channel of a story, I have made up my mind to get to work on one: always supposing that I find myself, on the trial, able to do well. Nothing whatever will do me the least 'good' in the way of shaking the one strong possession of change impending over us that every day makes stronger; but if I could work on with some approach to steadiness, through the summer, the anxious toil of a new book would have its neck well broken before beginning to publish, next October or November. Sometimes, I think I may continue to work; sometimes, I think not."

It was not until twelve months later, however, that he really commenced the tale which succeeded "Little Dorrit." During the interval *All the Year Round* had taken the place of *Household Words*, and the initial number of that weekly journal contained the first chapter of the new romance. It was a noteworthy innovation for a story by Charles Dickens to appear in a serial publication; but it must be remembered that it was also issued in monthly parts, each in the familiar green cover and containing two illustrations. This "rather original and bold idea," he explained to Mr. Forster, "will give *All the Year Round* always the interest and precedence of a fresh weekly portion during the month; and will give me my old standing with my old public, and the advantage (very necessary in this story) of having numbers of people who read it in no portions smaller than a monthly part." That the author fully realised the increased difficulty in writing a novel for publication in weekly instalments is indicated in a letter to a correspondent, where he pointed out how patiently and expressly a story like "A Tale of Two Cities" has to be planned for presentation in fragmentary form, and yet for afterwards fusing together as an uninterrupted whole—that there must be a special design to overcome that specially trying mode of publication.

Dickens conceived the main idea of "A Tale of Two Cities" while acting with his children and friends in Mr. Wilkie Collins's drama of "The Frozen Deep."

> "A strong desire was upon me then," he writes in the Preface, "to embody it in my own person; and I traced out in my fancy the state of mind of which it would necessitate the presentation to an observant spectator, with particular care and interest. As the idea became familiar to me, it gradually shaped itself into its present form. Throughout its execution, it has had complete possession of me; I have so far verified what is done and suffered in these pages, as that I have certainly done and suffered it all myself."

The author's first intention was to write this novel upon a plan proposed in his manuscript-book: "How as to a story in two periods—with a lapse of time between, like a French Drama?" The query is followed by a list of titles suitable for such a notion :—

"TIME! THE LEAVES OF THE FOREST. SCATTERED LEAVES. THE GREAT WHEEL. ROUND AND ROUND. OLD LEAVES. LONG AGO. FAR APART. FALLEN LEAVES. FIVE AND TWENTY YEARS. YEARS AND YEARS. ROLLING YEARS. DAY AFTER DAY. FELLED TREES. MEMORY CARTON. ROLLING STONES. TWO GENERATIONS."

Originally (that is, before the story was effectually grasped) he had suggested others: "What do you say to the title, ONE OF THESE DAYS?" This held its ground very briefly, and after six weeks he asked, "What do you think of *this* name for my story—BURIED ALIVE? Does it seem too grim? Or, THE THREAD OF GOLD? Or, THE DOCTOR OF BEAUVAIS?" At length, on March 11th, 1859, he certified that he had "got exactly the name for the story that is wanted; exactly what will fit the opening to a T. A TALE OF TWO CITIES."

The writing of the narrative did not begin under very auspicious circumstances, as the novelist was seriously handicapped by a sharp attack of illness. Happily, on July 9th, he was thus enabled to report progress: "I have been getting on in health very slowly and through irksome botheration enough. But I think I am round the corner. This cause—and the heat—has tended to my doing no more than hold my ground, my old month's advance, with the 'Tale of Two Cities.' The small portions thereof drive me frantic." It should be remembered that not only was he engaged upon the general editing of *All the Year Round*, but was simultaneously occupied with the first series of his Public Readings in London and the Provinces, both of which responsibilities must have greatly hampered him, and diverted his thoughts from the more important task. In order, however, to counteract the probable effect of these varied occupations, and desiring that his mind should be thoroughly imbued with his subject, Dickens read no books, while at work upon his romance, but such as had the air of the time in which the scenes in that dramatic novel are laid.

In "A Tale of Two Cities" he had set himself "the little task of making *a picturesque story*, rising in every chapter, with characters true to nature, but whom the story should express more than they should express themselves by dialogue"; in other words, he "fancied a story of incident might be written (in place of the odious stuff that *is* written under that pretence), pounding the characters in its own mortar, and beating their interest out of them." In the Preface he repeats that he hoped to add something to "the popular and picturesque means of understanding that terrible time" [the French Revolution], "though no one can hope to add anything to the philosophy of Mr. Carlyle's wonderful book."

Mr. J. T. Fields records that Dickens, when writing "A Tale of Two Cities," asked Carlyle if he might see one of the works to which he referred in his history; whereupon Carlyle packed up and sent down to Gad's Hill *all* his reference volumes, and Dickens read them faithfully.* Such a pleasant reminiscence well

* Dickens greatly admired the writings of Carlyle, and had especial reverence for "The French Revolution," which the novelist declared was the book of all others which he read perpetually and of which he never tired. He always found himself turning away from the volumes of reference, and re-reading with increased wonder that marvellous production. There is an interesting photographic group (by Mason and Co., 1865) representing Charles Dickens reading to his daughters on the lawn in front of the novelist's residence at Gad's Hill; the book which engages their attention is Carlyle's "French Revolution."

illustrates the care with which the novelist worked. Mr. Forster, in whose biography many instances of this thoughtful deliberation are given, draws attention to the fact that one of the proposed titles for the book (viz., "Memory Carton") shows that what led to its greatest success was always in his mind, while another memorandum appears in a rough hint of the character itself: "The drunken?—dissipated?—What?—LION—and his JACKALL and Primer, stealing down to him at unwonted hours." Respecting the novelist's treatment of another prominent character, Dr. Manette, Mr. Wilkie Collins (who liked the story so much) made a suggestion which Dickens could not see his way to adopt, the proposed emendation being, as he expressed it, "too elaborately trapped, baited, and prepared—in the main anticipated, and its interest wasted."

"Phiz," writing to one of his sons on the subject of "A Tale of Two Cities," says: "A rather curious thing happened with this book. Watts Phillips, the dramatist, hit upon the very same identical plot; they had evidently both of them been to the same source in Paris for their story. Watts' play came out with great success, with stunning climax, at about the same time of Dickens's sixth number. The public saw that they were identically the same story, so Dickens shut up at the ninth number instead of going on to the eighteenth as usual."*

It has been averred that Dickens, for the purposes of this novel, partly made use of the romance connected with the once famous firm of Thelluson. Like that of Tellson, the banking establishment of Thelluson had a very close relationship with Paris; indeed, we are told that Peter Thelluson had belonged to the Paris firm of Thelluson and Necker, the former migrating to London, where he successfully established a branch of the French business. There is also the more probable suggestion that another old-fashioned banking-house, that of Child in Fleet Street (rebuilt in 1878), was the actual prototype of Tellson's. The late Mr. Edmund Yates has pointed out that the character of Mr. Stryver was drawn from Mr. Edwin James, a well-known legal functionary some forty years ago. Mr. Yates says: "One day I took Dickens—who had never seen Edwin James—to one of these consultations. James

* *Century*, January, 1893. The story closed with the *eighth* number, and not the ninth, as stated by "Phiz."

laid himself out to be specially agreeable; Dickens was quietly observant. About four months after appeared the early numbers of 'A Tale of Two Cities,' in which a prominent part was played by Mr. Stryver. After reading the description, I said to Dickens: 'Stryver is a good likeness!' He smiled. 'Not bad, I think,' he said, 'especially after only one sitting.'"

"A Tale of Two Cities" was published in weekly instalments in *All the Year Round*, commencing with No. 1 of that periodical, dated April 30th, 1859, and ending in No. 31, on November 26th following. It was also issued concurrently in eight monthly parts by Messrs. Chapman and Hall, to whom the author now returned for the publication of the remainder of his books, of which he always in future reserved the copyrights; the size was demy octavo, with the usual green wrappers, the price of each number being one shilling. The first Part appeared in June and the last in December, Parts 7 and 8 forming a double number; the story contained sixteen etched illustrations by H. K. Browne, whose connection with Dickens, as illustrator, now came to an end. The complete work was published in December, 1859, in one volume, cloth, at nine shillings—pp. viii., one unnumbered page (List of Plates), and pp. 254—and was inscribed to Lord John Russell, "in remembrance of many public services and private kindnesses." The story has often been reissued, with or without a date. The first Cheap Edition was published by Messrs. Chapman and Hall in the Third Series, 1864, cloth, at five shillings, with a frontispiece by Marcus Stone, R.A.

A copy of the first edition, in numbers as issued, is valued at from £4 to £6; in cloth, £3. It is somewhat scarce, and an exceptionally fine impression was recently catalogued at twelve guineas. The original MS. is at South Kensington.

Writing to Mr. Forster in July, 1859, Dickens said: "The run upon our monthly parts is surprising, and last month we sold 35,000 back numbers." The demand for this essentially altruistic story in parts, however, could not have been so great as formerly, which is probably owing to the fact that it was appearing simultaneously in a cheaper form. It appears that Dickens's "American ambassador" (as he termed his Transatlantic publisher) paid him a thousand pounds for the first year for the privilege of republishing "A Tale of Two Cities" one day after it was issued in London. He informed his biographer, however, that "nothing in the way of mere money" could "repay the time and trouble of the incessant condensation" requisite for the particular method of publication; it was "the interest of the subject, and the pleasure of striving with the difficulty of the form of treatment," which really compensated him for the labour bestowed upon the tale.

On the completion of the tale Dickens intimated to M. Regnier that he hoped it was the best he had written; and to Mr. Wilkie Collins, "It has greatly moved and excited me in the doing, and Heaven knows I have done my best and believed in it." The novelist received a note from Carlyle about the book which gave him especial pleasure, and he was similarly gratified by an expression of appreciation from Lord Lytton, who discussed with the author certain points in the plot. The heroic personality of Sydney Carton undoubtedly constituted him a favourite with every reader. Dickens himself liked his conception of the character, and entertained "a faint idea sometimes that if I had acted him, I could have done something with his life and death." The entire story, and particularly Carton, was greatly admired by an American critic, Mr.

Richard Grant White, whose literary studies had most familiarised him with the rarest forms of imaginative writing; he pronounced it to be "so noble in its spirit, so grand and graphic in its style, and filled with a pathos so profound and simple, that it deserves and will surely take a place among the great serious works of imagination. The 'Tale of Two Cities,' his shortest story, and the one least thought of by the public of his own day, is the work that will secure him an enduring fame. . . . There is not a grander and lovelier figure than the self-wrecked, self-devoted Sydney Carton in literature or history." Mr. Forster considered the book as a really remarkable specimen of the novelist's power in imaginative story-telling, and Professor Ward contends that it holds a unique place among the fictions of its author—"an extraordinary *tour de force*, which Dickens never repeated."

In the *Saturday Review*, December 17th, 1859, a furious assault was made upon the story, the writer of this unreasonably savage article describing it as a most curious production, whether it is considered in a literary, in a moral, or in an historical point of view, and further vented his spleen by declaring that "if it had not borne Mr. Dickens's name, it would in all probability have hardly met with a single reader," etc., etc. An amusing report was current at the time that, as a result of reading this slashing indictment, Dickens was quite prostrated, remaining in bed for months in a state of helpless lethargy, and needing the constant application of warm flannels and bathings of mustard and turpentine, together with "the united influence of at least a dozen physicians, to restore him to consciousness"! The *Saturday Review*er notwithstanding, it is generally believed that, had the author of "A Tale of Two Cities" concentrated his attention upon the writing of picturesque historical novels, he could have created one of the greatest works of this nature ever published. Evidence of this is to be found, not only in his vivid picture of the Gordon Riots, but in various descriptive passages in his less-known production, "A Child's History of England."

It was, doubtless, principally owing to the dramatic qualities of "A Tale of Two Cities" that it needed but little alteration in order to be converted into an effective stage-play. As a matter of fact, Dickens actually sent the proof-sheets of the book to his friend M.

Regnier, with a view to ascertaining what he thought of the story being dramatised for a French theatre. There is, however, no evidence of this having been done; indeed, the tale of the Revolution and its sanguinary vengeance was unlikely to commend itself to the Imperial censorship. In England its reception would naturally prove more favourable, and we find that the novelist aided Mr. Tom Taylor in the dramatisation of his romance, the stage version of which he superintended in 1860, at the Lyceum Theatre, then under the management of Madame Céleste.

The late Mr. J. Waterson, formerly bandmaster of the 1st Life Guards, composed a Dramatic Overture, entitled "Lucie Manette," which was founded upon "A Tale of Two Cities." The description of the Overture, giving an epitome of the story, and printed on a separate leaflet, was written expressly for Mr. Waterson by Dickens himself—at least, so we are informed by the leaflet in question. It is elsewhere recorded that this musical composition was played in the band practice-room at Regent's Park in the presence of the novelist, who specially visited the barracks for the purpose of hearing the performance.

"GREAT [illegible]TATIONS."

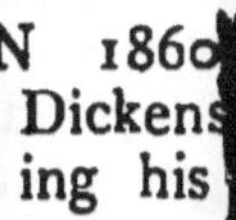N 1860 [illegible] suggested to Dickens [illegible]stead of occupying his [illegible] writing short papers [illegible]e *Year Round,* he should "let hi[illegible]se" upon some single humorous [illegible]n in the vein of his youthful ach[illegible]. In reply to this practical hi[illegible]d that such a very fine, new, a[illegible]sque idea had just opened upo[illegible] little piece he had nearly comp[illegible]t he began to doubt whether it [illegible] be preferable to cancel the brie[illegible]nd reserve the notion for a new [illegible]otion that was so vividly realised [illegible] that he could "see the whole of a[illegible]olving on it, in a most singular an[illegible]anner." This was the germ of [illegible]agwitch. At first he intended [illegible] it the groundwork of a tale in [illegible]twenty-number form, but the sta[illegible]ospects of *All the Year Round* [illegible] appears, been somewhat prejud[illegible]ffected by the

publication therein of a tale (Charles Lever's "A Day's Ride") which had disappointed expectation, and it was this which induced him to strengthen the position of that serial by another novel from his own pen. "I called a council of war at the office on Tuesday," he wrote to Mr. Forster (October 4th, 1860), in a letter intimating that he had got to work on the new romance. "It was perfectly clear that the one thing to be done was, for me to strike in. I have therefore decided to begin the story as of the length of the 'Tale of Two Cities' on the first of December—begin publishing, that is. I must make the most I can out of the book. . . . The name is GREAT EXPECTATIONS. I think a good name?" Two days later he wrote in further explanation: "The sacrifice of 'Great Expectations' is really and truly made for myself. The property of *All the Year Round* is far too valuable, in every way, to be much endangered. Our fall is not large, but we have a considerable advance in hand of the story we are now publishing, and there is no vitality in it, and no chance whatever of stopping the fall; which on the contrary would be certain to increase. Now, if I went into a twenty-number serial, I should cut off my power of doing anything serial here [illegible] good years—and that would be a most perilous thing. On the other hand, by dashing in now, I come in when most wanted."

During the latter part of September, 1860, the novelist commenced the writing of "Great Expectations," and a few days from that date brought Mr. Forster the first instalment, with the following forecast of the plan of the story and its plot: "The book will be written in the first person through[illegible] during these first three weekly n[illegible] you will find the hero to be a boy[illegible]ke David [Copperfield]. Then [illegible]be an apprentice. You will not have to complain of the want of humour, as in the 'Tale of Two Cities.' I have made the opening, I hope, in its general effect exceedingly droll. I have put a child and a good-natured foolish man, in relations that seem to me very funny. Of cou[illegible]e got in the pivot on which the [illegible]ll turn, too—and which, indeed, [illegible]emember, was the grotesque tragi[illegible]onception that first encouraged me[illegible]e quite certain he had fallen into [illegible]scious repetitions, Dickens read '[illegible]opperfield" again, and "was affe[illegible]t to a degree you would hardly b[illegible]

The first nu[illegible]peared on the 1st

of December, and on the 4th he thus wrote to Mr. A. H. Layard, declining an invitation from that gentleman to meet him: "A new story of my writing, nine months long, is just begun in *All the Year Round.* A certain allotment of my time when I have that story-demand upon me, has, all through my author life, been an essential condition of my health and success. I have just returned here [Gad's Hill Place] to work so many hours every day for so many days." There can be no doubt that, on going to reside at his Kentish home, his old love for the neighbourhood revived. "He again enjoyed the favourite rambles of his boyhood, gathering local colouring for his new novel principally from the ancient city of Rochester and the dreary neighbourhood of the marshes. In after-years he often walked with friends to Cooling, for the purpose of pointing out, in the churchyard there, the thirteen small tombstones of various sizes adapted to the respective ages of as many small children of one family ("Comport of Cowling Court, 1771") to which he referred in "Great Expectations," although in the story he makes the number of stone lozenges only five. The picturesque Elizabethan structure in Rochester known as "Restoration

House" had also a curious attraction for him, and he introduced it in the tale as Satis House *— [illegible] e of that extraordinary recluse, [illegible] visham.

In the openin [illegible] r of "Great Expectations" the [illegible] exciting scene among the mar [illegible] the chase and recapture of M [illegible] which has its parallel at the c [illegible] similar episode on the river, whe [illegible] elps the convict to escape. As [illegible] ce of Dickens's desire for accura [illegible] recorded that he hired a steamer [illegible] day in order to have a prelimina [illegible] of the Thames, to make sure o [illegible] ual course of a boat in such circ [illegible] s as described in the fifteenth cha [illegible] he third volume, and to discover [illegible] ssible incidents might arise. Se [illegible] nds, as well as members of his [illegible] ccompanied him on this unique [illegible] , and, although he seemed to th [illegible] othing but their enjoyment, his k [illegible] rvation was ever on the alert, not [illegible] ping his notice on either side of [illegible]

* There is actually [illegible] ouse in Rochester. Restoration House [illegible] d because it was here that Charles II. [illegible] en, on his restoration in 1660, he was [illegible] ed at a sumptuous banquet by the ma [illegible] corporation of the city.

This strikingly-pow [illegible] mance regu-
larly appeared at the [illegible] ed intervals
in *All the Year R* [illegible] The novelist
found that the plann [illegible] rom week to
week occasioned gr [illegible] culties, such
as (he declared) nob [illegible] imagine who
has not had the [illegible] ce; but he
realized that, as in a [illegible] cases, when
the trouble was ov [illegible] the pleasure
was proportionate. [illegible] before the
conclusion of the [illegible] e sent Mr.
Forster the chapters [illegible] pen the third
division of the tal [illegible] panied by an
expression of reg [illegible] at the third
portion cannot be [illegible] at once, because its purpose [illegible] e much more
apparent; and th [illegible] s the greater
because the gener [illegible] nd tone of the
working out and w [illegible] p, will be away
from all such thin [illegible] ey convention-
ally go. But wh [illegible] be, must be."
Another letter t [illegible] ght upon an
objection taken ([illegible] rly, Mr. Forster
considered) to th [illegible] eat speed with
which the heroi [illegible] being married,
reclaimed, and w [illegible] s made love to
and remarried by [illegible] o. Such a sum-
mary proceeding [illegible] er, was not originally intended, [illegible] e last few lines
the novelist had [illegible] at Pip remained
a solitary man. [illegible] Lytton, who was

privileged to read the proofs of the tale, objected to so sorrowful a conclusion, and strongly urged Dickens to change it by marrying Pip to Estella, supporting his view with such good reasons that the author resolved to make the suggested improvement. "I have put in as pretty a piece of writing as I could," he intimated to Mr. Forster, "and I have no doubt the story will be more acceptable through the alteration." Although Dickens himself thought that, upon the whole, the amendment was for the better, Mr. Forster considered that the first ending seemed to be more consistent with the drift, as well as natural working out, of the romance.*

The story terminated on August 3rd, 1861. Its publication in *All the Year Round* made a very great success of it, but, over and above its popular acceptance, the book was admired by those whose opinions Dickens highly valued. "It seems universally liked," he wrote to Miss Mary Boyle, December 28th, 1860. "I suppose because it opens funnily, and with an interest too." Carlyle used to ask impatiently for "that Pip nonsense" whenever the new number

* The close of "Great Expectations," as originally written, is preserved in a note in Forster's Life of Dickens, Vol. III., 336.

was due, although at first it was entirely put aside as not on any account to have time wasted over it. Bulwer Lytton, too, was extraordinarily taken with the tale, and made its author happy by what he said of it. "There is nothing like the pride of making such an effect on such a writer as you," remarked Dickens to his brother-novelist.

A well-known American critic, Mr. E. P. Whipple, in a review of the book, said: "There is much of Dickens's best writing in 'Great Expectations.' The characterisation is forcible even when it is least attractive. . . . The plot is more ingeniously complicated than any other of Dickens's novels except 'Bleak House.'" Mr. Forster, in his biography, expresses great admiration of the masterly drawing of character to be found in "Great Expectations," and further remarks that it may be doubted if Dickens could better have established his right to the front rank among novelists claimed for him, than by the ease and mastery with which, in "Copperfield" and "Great Expectations," he "kept perfectly distinct the two stories of a boy's childhood, both told in the form of autobiography."

It is interesting to learn that, within recent times, the mysterious Miss Havisham was actually realised in Hungary, where an eccentric Fräulein languished out of life after thirty years' romantic retirement from the world. She had been a young and lively girl, engaged to marry a man whom she dearly loved; but he discarded her because she attended a certain merry-making against his wish, and from that day the unhappy woman never passed the doors of her abode until she was carried to her grave. Mr. J. F. Dexter fancies that the original of Miss Havisham lived near Hyde Park, and that she was burned to death in her house. At all events, Dickens's portrait of this strange creature is not, after all, so very unreal or exaggerated. It is conjectured that, for the purposes of the story, the novelist partly availed himself of the wedding-breakfast incident related in *Household Words* in connection with an old and historic London tavern known as "Dirty Dick's," in Bishopsgate Street Without, now demolished. The real name of "Dirty Dick" was Nathaniel Bentley, whose bride died suddenly on the morning of the projected wedding, whereupon the room containing the banquet was ordered by the disconsolate bridegroom to be closed and sealed, never to be re-opened during his lifetime—a wish that was duly respected. We are also told that the refrain, "Beat it out, beat it out—Old Clem!" in which Pip and his friends indulged, is from a song which the blacksmiths in Chatham Dockyard used to sing in procession on St. Clement's Day.*

"Great Expectations" first appeared, in weekly instalments, in *All the Year Round*, commencing on December 1st, 1860, and ending on August 3rd, 1861. Directly after its conclusion in this periodical, it was published by Messrs. Chapman and Hall in three volumes, post octavo, cloth, at 31*s.* 6*d.*, and was inscribed to Chauncy Hare Townshend.† *Collation:* Vol. I., one unnumbered page (containing Inscription), pp. 344; Vol. II., pp. 351; Vol. III., pp. 344. No less than five editions were circulated in this form, none of them being illustrated. In the following year (1862) a New Edition, in one volume (post octavo, blue cloth, pp. 524) was published by the same firm; it contained a frontispiece and vignette by Marcus Stone, R.A., and the price was 7*s.* 6*d.* It has often been re-issued, with or without a date. The first

* *Vide* "A Week's Tramp in Dickens-Land," by W. R. Hughes, 1892.

† The "Religious Opinions of the late Rev. Chauncy Hare Townshend" were reduced to book form by Dickens, and published in 1869.

Cheap Edition (1863) was included in the Third Series, cloth, 5*s*., with a frontispiece by the above-mentioned artist.

Notwithstanding the fact that the first edition of "Great Expectations" contains no illustrations, the price demanded for a clean copy is from £7 to £10. This high figure is accounted for by the great scarcity of the three consecutive volumes in their original form, purchasers having sometimes to be content with making up the set with volumes of varying editions. The book, when first issued, was sold out immediately, the greater part of the impression going to the libraries; it was therefore looked upon with comparative disrespect, and, being immensely popular, became promptly thumbed, torn, and marked; whereas the weekly instalments in *All the Year Round* were preferred by private purchasers and collectors, who preserved them for binding. Mr. Wilkie Collins's copy of "Great Expectations" realised £9 5*s*. in the auction-room, at the sale of his library in 1890.

As in the case of his previous work, "A Tale of Two Cities," Dickens received from America a thousand pounds for early proofs of the story, that arrangement having been made prior to its publication in England.

The original MS. of "Great Expectations" is in the Museum at Wisbech, Cambs. It was presented by Dickens (together with a copy of the book) to the Rev. Chauncy Hare Townshend in July, 1861, by whom it was bequeathed to the Wisbech Museum, where it was deposited in 1868. The whole of the manuscript is written in a very small hand, and is full of corrections.

"OUR MUTUAL FRIEND."

MR. FORSTER, responding to the toast "The Interests of Literature" at the Royal Academy banquet on May 1st, 1864, gracefully alluded to Charles Dickens (who was present) as "the great master of character and humour who has held sway over both now for more than a quarter of a century, and this very day starts after new laurels with as much vigour and freshness as when he first began the race." The work to which he referred was "Our Mutual Friend," the first instalment being published on the above date. The novelist had chosen his title two years previously, and, believing it to be a good one, held to it through much objection. The following explanatory note was inserted in one of the early numbers: "The Reader will understand the use of the popular phrase Our Mutual

Friend, as the title of this book, on arriving at the Ninth Chapter (page 84)." This title (which, by the way, is held to be partly responsible for the extinction of the phrase of which it consists) gave rise to considerable controversy at the time, many arguing that the adjective "mutual" was incorrect. It may be mentioned that in his book of memoranda Dickens had written several titles for future novels, and in this list will be found some that were evidently intended for the present story, viz., "Rokesmith's Forge," "The Cinder Heap," "Broken Crockery," "Dust."

In his letters at this time Dickens mentioned three leading notions on which he founded the tale, the most noteworthy being that which was the outcome of the many handbills which he saw posted up during his waterside wanderings; these contained dreary descriptions of persons drowned in the river, and suggested to his mind the long-shore men and their ghastly calling, as graphically sketched in Hexam and Riderhood. "I think," he wrote on one occasion, "a man, young and perhaps eccentric, feigning to be dead, and *being* dead to all intents and purposes, external to himself, and for years retaining the singular view of life and character so imparted, would be a good leading incident for a story"; and this idea was partly carried out in Rokesmith. For other personages in the tale he had in view "a poor impostor of a man marrying a woman for her money; she marrying *him* for *his* money; after marriage both finding out their mistake, and entering into a league and covenant against folks in general." With these he had proposed to connect some "perfectly new" people, who should have everything new about them; "if they presented a father and mother, it seemed as if THEY must be bran new, like the furniture and the carriages—shining with varnish, and just home from the manufacturers." This conception was realized in the Lammles and Veneerings; while Charley Hexam and his father were suggested by "the uneducated father in fustian and the educated boy in spectacles" whom he and John Leech had seen at Chatham.

The manuscript note-book again proved serviceable in supplying hints for "Our Mutual Friend." In it were jotted down some studies of Silas Wegg and his patron, even more comical in conception, it seems, than they were afterwards rendered in the story. Here, also, are the following memoranda:—

"Gibbon's Decline and Fall. The two characters. One reporting to the other as he reads. Both getting confused as to whether it is not all going on now." [Then comes a suggestion for Bella Wilfer and parent.] "Buying poor shabby—FATHER?—a new hat. So incongruous that it makes him like African King Boy, or King George; who is usually full dressed when he has nothing upon him but a cocked hat or a waistcoat." [Then a hint of Podsnap's traits.] "I stand by my friends and acquaintances;—not for their sakes, but because they are *my* friends and acquaintances. *I* know them, *I* have licensed them, they have taken out *my* certificate. Ergo, I champion them as myself. . . . And by denying a thing, supposes that he altogether puts it out of existence." [Here is the first thought for Eugene Wrayburn's mischievous assistant.] "The office-boy for ever looking out of window, who never has anything to do." [The germ of good-natured Eugene Wrayburn himself is now indicated.] "If they were great things, I, the untrustworthy man in little things, would do them earnestly——But O No, I wouldn't! . . . As to the question whether I, Eugene, lying ill and sick even unto death, through this illness, I shall begin a new life, and have energy and purpose and all I have yet wanted: '*I hope* I should, but *I know* I shouldn't. Let me die, my dear.'"* [Then

* Mr. Marcus Stone, R.A., informs me that the novelist at first intended Eugene Wrayburn should die when assaulted by the schoolmaster, but afterwards changed his mind.

we have a notion from which, though not otherwise worked out in the tale, the relation of Lizzie Hexam to her brother was derived.] "A man, and his wife—or daughter—or niece. The man, a reprobate and ruffian; the woman (or girl) with good in her, and with compunctions. He believes nothing, and defies everything; yet has suspicions always, that she is 'praying against' his evil schemes, and making them go wrong. He is very much opposed to this, and is always angrily harping on it. 'If she *must* pray, why can't she pray in their favour, instead of going against 'em? She's always ruining me—she always is—and calls that, Duty! There's a religious person! Calls it Duty to fly in my face! Calls it Duty to go sneaking against me!'"

The latter portion of these notes evidently has reference to Jerry Cruncher, in "A Tale of Two Cities." "Other fancies preserved in the memoranda," remarks Mr. Forster, "were left wholly unemployed, receiving from the author no more permanent form of any kind than that which they have in this touching record. What most people would probably think the most attractive and original of all the thoughts he had thus set down for future use are those that were never used."

Dickens hoped to have begun "Our Mutual Friend" directly he had satisfied himself as to the title. The time required for the second series of his Public Readings, which took place between October, 1861, and June, 1862, is probably one reason why the wish was not consummated, while another and very plausible explanation is that he could think of no definite plot for the story, notwithstanding repeated attempts to conceive something suitably striking and novel. He had at this time temporarily exchanged Gad's Hill Place for a friend's residence at Kensington, and the "odious little house" [he wrote] "seems to have stifled and darkened my invention." It was not until the autumn of 1863 that he saw his way to a beginning, when he described himself as being "full of notions for the new twenty numbers," and hoping, when his Christmas work on *All the Year Round* was over, to "dash into it on the grander journey." Being exceedingly anxious about his book, he even endeavoured to shirk his editorial labours in order that he might be better able to concentrate attention upon it in the quietude of his Gad's Hill retreat. Presently he wrote: "I see my opening perfectly, with the one main line on which the story is to turn; and if I don't strike while the iron (meaning myself) is hot, I shall drift off again, and have to go all through this uneasiness once more." On January 24th, 1864, he wrote to Mr. Wilkie Collins: "I have done the two first numbers, and am beginning the third. It is a combination of drollery with romance which requires a great deal of pains and a perfect throwing away of points that might be amplified; but I hope it is *very good.* I confess, in short, that I think it is. Strange to say, I felt at first quite dazed in getting back to the large canvas and the big brushes; and even now, I have a sensation as of acting at the San Carlo after Tavistock House, which I could hardly have supposed would have come upon so old a stager."

He was determined not to begin to publish with less than five numbers completed, and had written very nearly three when, upon a necessary re-arrangement of his chapters, he hit upon a new subject for one of them. This was the quaint establishment (No. 42, St. Andrew Street, near Seven Dials) of a taxidermist and articulator of human bones, to which the illustrator of the story, Mr. Marcus Stone, had directed his attention, the description of which took the place of the last chapter of No. 2, this being then transferred to the end of No. 3. The proprietor's name was Willis, and when Mr. Percy Fitzgerald next saw the novelist, he said: "I am convinced I have found the original of 'Venus'"; on which said Mr. Dickens, "You are right!" The place could at once be recognised at the time the book appeared.

Although the novelist had much material in hand for his story, he progressed slowly and painfully. "If I were to lose," he wrote on March 29th, "a page of the five numbers I have proposed to myself to be ready by the publication day, I should feel that I had fallen short. I have grown hard to satisfy, and write very slowly. And I have so much—not fiction—that *will* be thought of, when I don't want to think of it, that I am forced to take more care than I once took." This excessive caution was significant of a change, both mental and physical; he was working too hard, and the strain of the Public Readings was beginning seriously to tell upon him.

On May 1st, the initial number of "Our Mutual Friend" was launched, and two days later Dickens joyfully announced that the sale was then in its 30th thousand, "and orders flowing in fast." This success was unfortunately not maintained, there being a distinct falling-off in the demand for Part 2; however, before the book closed the larger number was again reached. The variation in the extent of the sales of the first two instalments seems to have somewhat undecided the author, for on June 10th he wrote: "This leaves me going round and round like a carrier-pigeon before swooping on number seven." In addition to worries thus entailed, there was a return of illness, and on July 29th he wrote sadly: "Although I have not been wanting in industry, I have been wanting in invention, and have fallen back with the book." After referring to being "out of sorts," he expressed a fear that he would lose ground, "and, as I know from two days' slow experience, have a very mountain to climb before I shall see the open country of my work." The death at this time of his old friend John Leech, too, put him out woefully, and he seemed for the nonce to have quite lost the power of writing. Presently he rallied, but in February, 1865, he experienced a formidable affection of the foot, and consequent lameness compelled him to abstain from his favourite walking exercise. In April he was staying at 16, Somer's Place, Hyde Park, where, although suffering severely, he continued to work "like a dragon" at his book, and was (as he informed Macready) "a terror to the household, likewise to all organs and brass bands in this quarter." Anxiety and ill-health necessitated a complete change, and after trying the sea he decided to go abroad, fully realising that work and worry would soon make an end of him. "If I were not going away now," he wrote, "I should break down. No one knows as I know to-day how near to it I have been."

After a brief sojourn in France, whither he went for the needful rest, his health had decidedly improved. But a dreadful shock was in store for him—that most terrible experience, the Staplehurst railway accident of June 9th, 1865. Dickens was in the fated train on his way home; a bridge had collapsed, and the carriage in which he travelled hung down the side of a chasm in an inexplicable manner. With great presence of mind, the novelist released himself from this dangerous position, and with great energy worked away for hours among the dying and dead, his efforts being handsomely acknowledged afterwards by the directors of the Company. Although not bodily injured, Dickens felt the effects of that fearful day for a considerable time, as his correspondence proves, and could never again travel on the railway without great mental anguish. He still remained curiously weak, as though recovering from a long illness, and was unable to indite half-a-dozen notes without turning faint and sick. "I am getting right, though still low in pulse and very nervous," was the report of his physical condition at this period, the result being that he could not keep up to time with his novel. "Alas!" he said to Mr. Forster at the opening of July, "for the two numbers you write of! There is only one in existence. I have but just begun the other." "Fancy!" he observed next day, "fancy my having under-written number sixteen by two and a-half pages—a thing I have not done since 'Pickwick'!" He did it once with "Dombey," however, and was to do it yet again.

A portion of the manuscript of "Our Mutual Friend," viz., the chapters he had written during his brief stay in France, was in his possession at the time of the Staplehurst disaster, when author and "copy" so nearly perished. This fact is thus alluded to by Dickens in the "Post-script in lieu of Preface" (dated 2nd of

September, 1865), which accompanied the last number :—

"On Friday the ninth of June in the present year, Mr. and Mrs. Boffin (in their manuscript dress of receiving Mr. and Mrs. Lammle at breakfast) were on the South-Eastern Railway with me, in a terribly destructive accident. When I had done what I could to help others, I climbed back into my carriage—nearly turned over a viaduct, and caught aslant upon the turn—to extricate the worthy couple. They were much soiled, but otherwise unhurt. The same happy result attended Miss Bella Wilfer on her wedding-day, and Mr. Riderhood inspecting Bradley Headstone's red neckerchief as he lay asleep. I remember with devout thankfulness that I can never be much nearer parting company with my readers for ever, than I was then, until there shall be written against my life the two words with which I have this day closed my book—THE END."

With shaken nerves, but with energy unsubdued, the writing of "Our Mutual Friend" was continued until its completion, the final instalment (a double number) being published in November, 1865. It is said that at the last moment, while the manuscript was in the printers' hands, Dickens decided to re-write a whole chapter that was already in type, and this he did, in the very greatest haste and excitement, while the firm's senior reader waited for it. Produced under such adverse circumstances, it is hardly surprising that the story should fail to rank with his higher achievements. Mr. Forster, while admiring the pourtrayal of Jenny Wren as one of Dickens's masterpieces, considered that the book, as a whole, wants freshness and natural development, and has not the creative power which marked his earlier writings.

During the publication of "Oliver Twist," a Jewish lady remonstrated with Dickens on an injustice to the Jews as shown in the character of Fagin; in a subsequent letter, acknowledging a reply from Dickens, this lady argued that, though all the other criminal characters in the story are Christians (as the novelist had pointed out), they are at least contrasted with characters of good Christians, whereas Fagin stands alone as the Jew. The answer to this remonstrance was the conception of Riah, the benevolent old Jew in "Our Mutual Friend," which, together with other favourable sketches of Jewish character in *All the Year Round*, was intended to wipe out the reproach against Fagin as a type of the Hebrew race. The Jewish lady, however, was dissatisfied even with the presentment of Riah, and again wrote to Dickens, giving her reasons for the objections raised. Her letter brought a courteous reply from the novelist, in the course of which he said: "The error you point out to me had occurred to me, as most errors do to most people, when it was too late to correct it. But it will do no harm. The peculiarities of dress and manner are fused together for the sake of picturesqueness." More than two years had elapsed when Dickens became the recipient of a copy of Benicsh's Hebrew and English Bible, with this inscription: "Presented to Charles Dickens, in grateful and admiring recognition of his having exercised the noblest quality man can possess—that of atoning for an injury as soon as conscious of having inflicted it." This act of kind thoughtfulness was highly esteemed by the novelist, whose grateful note of thanks to the donor pleasantly closed an interesting incident in his literary career.

Mr. Percy Fitzgerald assures us that Mr. Podsnap is a veritable portrait of Dickens's biographer, and quotes certain passages in this attractive romance as being faithful delineations of the "actual living Forster"! The "mutual friend" in the story is John Harmon, *alias* Julius Handford, *alias* John Rokesmith. The prototype of Mr. Boffin, the Golden Dustman, was a wealthy philanthropist named

Henry Dodd, with whom Dickens was personally acquainted. He was a London contractor on a large scale, and owned an enormous dust-heap in Shepherdess Fields, Islington. Being passionately fond of the play, he endowed several dramatic charities, but his pet project of founding a dramatic college unfortunately collapsed by reason of its being based upon a wrong principle, after incurring the expenditure of very large subscriptions, and securing the patronage of the Queen. It is recorded that the opulent contractor presented to his daughter, as a wedding gift, one of his dust-heaps, which afterwards realised £10,000!

It was at the Children's Hospital in Great Ormond Street where the novelist found a pathetic setting for the death-bed of little Johnny (the orphan whom the Boffins proposed to adopt) in one of the quiet wards among the baby sufferers. It must have gratified Dickens to know that the result of the publication of "Our Mutual Friend" was a steady flow of subscriptions to that deserving institution, then badly needing support and interest.

"Our Mutual Friend" was issued by Messrs. Chapman and Hall in twenty monthly parts, green wrappers, demy octavo, at one shilling each, commencing in May, 1864, and ending in November, 1865—Parts 19 and 20 forming a double number. It contains forty woodcut illustrations by Marcus Stone, R.A. The complete work was published in November, in two volumes, cloth, at twenty-two shillings, with an Inscription to Sir James Emerson Tennent. *Collation:* Vol. I., pp. xi., 320; Vol. II., pp. viii., 309. It has often been reissued, with or without a date. The first Cheap Edition (being fifth of the Third Series) appeared in 1867, cloth, at five shillings (Messrs. Chapman and Hall), and contains a frontispiece by A. B. Houghton.

The cost of a copy of the first edition, even in the finest state of preservation, does not exceed from 25*s.* to 30*s.*, so that this particular work has not yet attained a high price. It should include the slip upon which is printed the explanatory Note already alluded to.

The original MS. of "Our Mutual Friend" has found a resting-place in America, whither so many Dickens treasures have departed. When the story first came out, Mr. E. S. Dallas, a prominent literary critic, wrote an appreciative review of it for the *Times*, which pleased the novelist exceedingly, and had the effect of largely increasing the sale of the book. In grateful acknowledgment, Dickens presented the manuscript to Mr. Dallas, who disposed of it shortly after the author's death to Mr. J. C. Hotten, a London publisher, at whose demise in 1874 it became the property of Mr. Welford, of *Scribner's*, and was through him sold to the late Mr. George Washington Childs, of Philadelphia, for £250. The sheets are mounted, and the whole bound up in two large quarto volumes. *Scribner's Monthly Magazine* for August, 1874, contains an interesting article (contributed anonymously by an American writer, the late Miss Kate Field, author of "Pen Photographs of Charles Dickens's Readings") on the subject of this manuscript. After describing the peculiarity of the handwriting and the novelist's method of erasing and correcting, Miss Field transcribes some of the more striking of the notes by Dickens which precede the novel in each volume; for it seems that, after thinking out his plot and characters, the author put down on the right-hand side of the page the chapters with *dramatis personæ*, while on the left were similarly inscribed his intentions respecting them, these memoranda proving that Dickens first conceived a plan of his story, and then made a skeleton of it from which to work in the details. The South Kensington authorities, desiring to complete their collection of Dickens manuscripts, offered the late Mr. Childs the sum of £1,200 for that of "Our Mutual Friend"; but the offer was courteously refused. Respecting this interesting relic of the famous novelist, Mrs. Childs writes: "The final destination of 'Our Mutual Friend' is with Mr. Childs's collection of MSS. at the Drexel Institute, Philadelphia."

"THE MYSTERY OF EDWIN DROOD."

THERE is naturally a pathetic interest attaching to this, the last, work of Charles Dickens, whose premature death unhappily prevented the completion of what promised to be one of his most dramatic efforts in literature. While preparing the early numbers of "Edwin Drood," the novelist was engaged upon his Farewell Readings, these taking place in London at intervals during January, February, and March, 1870. It is generally conceded that the excitement and fatigue incidental to these Readings indubitably hastened the end; *à propos* of which Mr. Ruskin wrote four years afterwards, in reply to an invitation to lecture: "The miserable death of poor Dickens, when he might have been writing blessed books till he was eighty, but for the pestiferous demand of the mob, is a very solemn warning to us all, if we would take it." In order to avoid the mental anguish which, when travelling on the railway, the novelist invariably experienced after the Staplehurst accident, he temporarily left Gad's Hill to take up his residence in the town house of his friend Mr. Milner Gibson, at 5, Hyde Park Place. Here, in a bedroom which commanded a splendid view of the Park, much of "Edwin Drood" was written; although the roar of Oxford Street beneath made itself very obvious, he was not affected by it, being singularly unsusceptible to noise.

Dickens began the writing of his final romance long before the publication of the initial part, being anxious to spare himself by having several instalments ready in advance. A hint of his first fancy for the tale was given to his biographer in July, 1869: "What should you think," he wrote, "of the idea of a story beginning in this way?—Two people, boy and girl, or very young, going apart from one another, pledged to be married after many years—at the end of the book. The interest to arise out of the tracing of their separate ways, and the impossibility of telling what will be done with that impending fate." Although this notion was laid aside, it left a marked trace on the story, as indicated in the rendering of the hero and his betrothed. A short tale Dickens had received for *All the Year Round*, entitled "An Experience" (published in the 37th number of the New Series), suggested an alteration of plot. "I laid aside the fancy I told you of," he wrote in August, "and have a very curious and new idea for my new story. Not a communicable idea (or the interest of the book would be gone), but a very strong one, though difficult to work." The story was to be that of the murder of a nephew by his uncle, and its originality was to consist in the review of the murderer's career by himself at the close, the last chapters to be written in the "condemned" cell to which his wickedness had brought him. Soon after the commission of the deed, the murderer was to realise the utter needlessness of it to secure his object; and all discovery of the murderer was to be baffled until near the close of the tale, when, by means of a gold ring which had resisted the corrosive effects of the lime into which he had thrown the body, not only the victim was to be identified, but also the locality of the crime and the perpetrator of it.* It will be remembered that the

* Such an incident as that here referred to actually happened in Rochester many years

ring, to be given by Drood to his betrothed only if their engagement continued, was brought away with him at their last interview; Rosa was to marry Tartar, and Crisparkle the sister of Landless, who (says Mr. Forster, in his recollections of the proposed course of the plot) was to have perished in assisting Tartar finally to unmask and seize the murderer. It has been surmised that Dickens studied a portion of a curious American work, entitled "Footfalls on the Boundary of Another World," by R. Owen (1860), with a view to supernatural events in the story.

The plan for the first number of "Edwin Drood" was thus briefly indicated: "Mr. Sapsea. Old Tory jackass. Connect Jasper with him. (He will want a solemn donkey by and by)"; which was effected by bringing together both Durdles and Jasper, for connection with Sapsea, in

ago. An inhabitant of the town was appointed trustee and guardian of his nephew, who went to sea, and eventually returned to his uncle's house. The young seafarer then mysteriously disappeared, and nothing more was heard of him. The uncle died, and when the house in which he resided underwent certain alterations in order to render it suitable for other purposes, a human skeleton was discovered, supposed to have been that of the missing nephew.

the matter of the epitaph for Mrs. Sapsea's tomb. The last of the memoranda, and the final words written by Dickens in the note-book containing them, are these: "'Then I'll give up snuff.' Brobity.—An alarming sacrifice. Mr. Brobity's snuff-box. The Pawnbroker's account of it?" As Mr. Forster says, "What was proposed by this must he left to conjecture; but 'Brobity' is the name of one of the people in his unfinished story, and the suggestion may have been meant for some incident in it. If so, it is the only passage in the volume which can be in any way connected with the piece of writing on which he was last engaged."

It appears that this romance gave its author more trouble than any of his former novels. His thoughts did not flow so freely as of yore; he revised and corrected his work continually, and sometimes entirely remodelled his sentences. Nor was he so successful as usual in estimating the amount of "copy" required for each number, the result, probably, of such excessive correction and interlineation. On December 22nd, 1869, he remarked: "When I had written, and, as I thought, disposed of the first two Numbers of my story, Clowes informed me to my horror that they were, together, *twelve printed pages too short!!!* Consequently I had to transpose a chapter from number two to number one, and remodel number two altogether." He completed the first Part during the third week of October, 1869, and on the 26th read it at Mr. Forster's house "with great spirit." The author experienced a keen pleasure in the story as the plot developed, and in a letter to his American friend, Mr. J. T. Fields (January 14th, 1870), he wrote: "There is a curious interest steadily working up to No. 5, which requires a great deal of art and self-denial. I think also, apart from character and picturesqueness, that the young people are placed in a very novel situation. So I hope—at Nos. 5 and 6 the story will turn upon an interest suspended until the end." Little did he then anticipate that, for him, alas! the end was rapidly approaching—that the ingenious plot he had mentally evolved would never be divulged.

Although suffering seriously at times from local hæmorrhage and a recurrence of the trouble in his foot, Dickens enjoyed intervals of comparative freedom from pain; indeed, on the morning of June 8th, 1870—the eve of "that sorrowful day"—he was in excellent spirits, talking to Miss Hogarth about his book, at which he was working in the pretty Swiss *châlet*, amongst the trees in his garden at Gad's Hill Place, leaving it once about noontime to smoke a cigar in the conservatory. It was during dinner that the fatal seizure came. All human help was unavailing, and on the evening of Thursday June 9th he passed away peacefully in his 59th year, leaving the world to mourn the loss of one who had delighted millions of readers—the great English novelist who had so often cheered them in their sorrow, sympathised with them in their joy, championed them when harassed by notorious social abuses. Shortly before his death, he was walking with a dear friend, when the latter, speaking of "Edwin Drood," remarked: "Well, you, or we, are approaching the mystery——" The novelist, who had been, and was at the moment, all vivacity, extinguished his gaiety, and fell into a long and silent reverie, from which he never broke during the remainder of the walk. Was he pondering another and deeper mystery than any his brain could unravel, facile as its mastery was over the hearts and brains of his brethren?*

During the publication of "Edwin

* *Vide* "A Day with Charles Dickens," by Blanchard Jerrold, 1872.

Drood," a letter was received by Dickens from Mr. J. M. Makeham, who therein referred to a passage in the tenth chapter of the story, respecting which he suggested that the novelist had, perhaps, forgotten that the figure of speech alluded to by him, "in a way which was distasteful to some of his admirers, was drawn from a passage of Holy Writ which is greatly reverenced by a large number of his countrymen as a prophetic description of the sufferings of our Saviour." [The passage referred to reads thus: ". . . would the Reverend Septimus submissively be led, like the highly-popular lamb who has so long and unresistingly been led to the slaughter, and there would he, unlike that lamb, bore nobody but himself."] To this Dickens replied, in one of the very last letters he wrote :—

"DEAR SIR,—It would be quite inconceivable to me—but for your letter—that any reasonable reader could possibly attach a scriptural reference to a passage in a book of mine, reproducing a much-abused social figure of speech, impressed into all sorts of service, on all sorts of inappropriate occasions, without the faintest connection of it with its original source. I am truly shocked to find that any reader can make the mistake. I have always striven in my writings to express veneration for the life and lessons of our Saviour; because I feel it; and because I rewrote that history for my children—every one of whom knew it from having it repeated to them, long before they could read, and almost as soon as they could speak. But I have never made proclamation of this from the house-tops.

"Faithfully yours,

"CHARLES DICKENS."

Longfellow, on hearing of the death of the famous English fictionist, immediately wrote to Mr. Forster expressing a hope that his book was finished. "It is certainly one of his most beautiful works," added the poet, "if not the most beautiful of all. It would be too sad to think the pen had fallen from his hand, and left it incomplete!" This generous praise found a warm supporter in Mr. Forster himself, who considered that "some of the characters in the story were touched with subtlety, and in its description his imaginative power was at its best. Not a line was wanting to the reality, in the most minute detail, of places the most widely contrasted; and we saw with equal vividness the lazy cathedral town and the lurid opium-eater's den."

How little Dickens suspected that his wonderful career was drawing to a close is shown by the fact that in his last letter to the manager of *All the Year*

Round, Mr. Holdsworth, written the day before his death, he asked him to purchase at "one of those Great Queen Street shops" a writing-slope for Gad's Hill, such as he had in use at the office. The slope hitherto used by him was presented as a memento of the deceased novelist to his friend Mr. Edmund Yates. At the latter's death in 1895 it was sold at Messrs. Sotheby's rooms for a hundred guineas, the purchaser being Mr. S. B. Bancroft, the well-known actor, who generously presented it to the South Kensington Museum. This unique relic of the most popular novelist of the age has since been added to the Forster Collection of Dickens MSS.

In the final instalment of "Edwin Drood" appeared the following Postscript by Messrs. Chapman and Hall:—

"All that was left in manuscript of EDWIN DROOD is contained in the Number now published —the sixth. Its last entire page had not been written two hours when the event occurred which one very touching passage in it (grave and sad, but also cheerful and assuring) might seem almost to have anticipated. The only notes in reference to the story that have since been found concern that portion of it exclusively which is treated in the earlier Numbers. Beyond the clues therein afforded to its conduct or catastrophe, nothing whatever remains; and it is believed that what the author himself would have most desired is done, in placing before the reader without further note or suggestion the fragment of THE MYSTERY OF EDWIN DROOD.

"*12th August*, 1870."

When making pecuniary arrangements respecting "The Mystery of Edwin Drood," it was agreed that the sum to be paid at once for 25,000 copies was £7,500, publishers and author sharing equally in the profit of all sales beyond that impression; in addition to which the sum of £1,000 was to be paid for advance sheets sent to America. Dickens especially stipulated by deed that Messrs. Chapman and Hall should be reimbursed for any possible loss that might accrue to them should he be prevented by death or sickness from completing the work. It was the first time such a clause had been inserted in one of his agreements, but it proved sadly pertinent in this case. The demand for "Edwin Drood" was eminently satisfactory. "We have been doing wonders with No. 1," he wrote to Mr. Fields on April 18th, 1870. "*It has very, very far outstripped every one of its predecessors.*" The number attained during the author's lifetime was 50,000.

Various reports were circulated at the time that the novel would be finished by other hands, and in 1882 the rumour was revived to the effect that Mr. Wilkie Collins was engaged in completing it; it was further intimated that he had been asked to bring the story to a conclusion, but declined doing so. Such erroneous statements were promptly denied by Messrs. Chapman and Hall, who, in a letter to the *Times*, announced that the deceased novelist had finished three numbers in addition to the three already published, and declared that, as no other writer could be permitted by them to complete the work, it would remain a fragment. It was hoped that Dickens had left among his papers a clue to the remaining portion of the plot, but it transpired that nothing had been written of the main parts of the design except what is found in the published numbers, nor could there be discovered a hint as to the author's intentions respecting the sequel. It was all a blank, although Mr. Forster, when engaged upon his Life of the novelist, believed he had stumbled upon a solution of the plot in some pages of nearly illegible manuscript, which, however, proved to be a scene in which Sapsea was introduced as the principal figure among a group of new characters.* Concerning this Mr. Forster suggests that Dickens, "having become a little nervous about the course of the tale, from a fear that he might have plunged too soon into the incidents leading on to the catastrophe," conceived the idea of opening some fresh veins of character incidental to the interest of the story.

Serious attempts have been made to solve the mystery of "Edwin Drood." The most noteworthy experiment is that of the late Mr. R. A. Proctor, F.R.A.S., whose little volume entitled "Watched by the Dead: A Loving Study of Charles Dickens's half-told Tale," 1887,† indicates that the author had attentively studied the romance; reasoning from certain data, he points out the probable fate of certain characters in the story, and concludes that Jasper was watched by Edwin Drood in the person of Datchery, and thus he was to have been tracked remorselessly "to his death by the man whom he supposed he had slain." Mr. Thomas Foster has also earnestly essayed, in a series of

* This scene is given in Forster's Life of Dickens, Vol. III., 433-9.

† An article on the same subject, also by Mr. Proctor, was published in the *Manchester Examiner*, August 1st, 1888.

articles, to point out the general direction of the path along which the story was to be conducted, and its final goal;* while an anonymous writer in the *Cornhill Magazine*, March, 1884, offers suggestions for a conclusion. Mr. Luke Fildes, R.A., the illustrator of the story, is convinced that Dickens intended Edwin Drood should be killed by his uncle—an opinion strengthened by the admission of Mr. Charles Dickens the Younger, whom the novelist himself informed that Drood was dead. Other interesting indications as to the plot are made by Mr. Fildes, who, from his artistic association with the story, is naturally enabled to throw light upon the subject, although he can but furnish a solitary missing-link. It seems that, while engaged upon the illustrations, he was so shrewd in his guesses respecting the "mystery" that Dickens became afraid he would be unable to keep the public from anticipating the point he was endeavouring so carefully to conceal. Mr. Charles Collins, the designer of the cover, was unconscious of the meaning of his designs, having produced them under the novelist's directions.

* *Belgravia*, June, 1878; "Leisure Readings," 1882; and *Knowledge*, September 12th to November 14th, 1884.

A prominent feature of "Edwin Drood" is the graphic account of opium-dens and their frequenters, which are still to be found in the East End of London. Dickens's American friend, Mr. J. T. Fields, has recorded that, during his stay in England in the summer of 1869, he accompanied the novelist one night (under police escort) to some lock-up houses, watch-houses, and opium-dens, it being from one of the latter that he gathered the incidents which are related in the opening pages. "In a miserable court," says Mr. Fields, "we found the haggard old woman blowing at a kind of pipe made of an old penny ink-bottle.* The identical words which Dickens puts into the mouth of this wretched creature in 'Edwin Drood' we heard her croon as we leaned over the tattered bed on which she was lying. There was something hideous in the way this woman kept repeating "Ye'll pay up according, deary, won't ye?' and the Chinamen and Lascars

* Mr. James Platt, jun., of St. Martin's Lane, who was personally acquainted with the old woman and her surroundings, declares that the pipe was a "scratch" one, made out of an old flageolet and a door-knob, the latter serving as a bowl, which Mr. Fields mistook for an ink-bottle.

made never-to-be-forgotten pictures in the scene." We also have Dickens's statement that what he described he saw—exactly as he had described it—down in Shadwell in the autumn of 1869. "A couple of the Inspectors of Lodging-houses knew the woman, and took me to her as I was making a round with them, to see for myself the working of Lord Shaftesbury's Bill." Relative to his sketch of opium-smoking, Sir John Bowring (who had been British Ambassador to China and Governor of Hong-Kong) pointed out to Dickens what appeared to him an inaccuracy in his delineation of that scene, and sent him an original Chinese sketch of the form of the pipe and the manner of its employment. While thanking him for the information, the novelist replied that he had only chronicled what actually came under his own observation in the neighbourhood of the London docks. Sir John's comment upon this is as follows: "No doubt the Chinaman whom he [Dickens] described had accommodated himself to English usage, and that our great and faithful dramatist here as elsewhere most correctly pourtrayed a piece of actual life."

Dickens placed the scene of Jasper's opium-smokings in a court just beyond the churchyard of St. George's-in-the-East, Stepney. The Rev. Harry Jones, rector from 1873 to 1882, mentions that the old crone was known as Lascar Sal, and was living at the time he wrote (1875). The John Chinaman of whom she was so jealous in her trade was George Ah Sing, who died in 1889; he resided at 131, Cornwall Road, St. George's-in-the-East, and at the inquest it transpired that death was due to the rupture of a blood-vessel accelerated by destitution. When the novelist visited him, he kept an opium-den in New Court, Victoria Street, E., which used to be a house of call for Chinese seamen coming to this country and others who indulged in the use of the drug. The particular den described in the story was pulled down some years ago to make room for a Board-school playground, while the bedstead, pipes, etc., were purchased by Americans and others interested in curious relics.

The picture of the Nuns' House in "Edwin Drood" was inspired by a sixteenth-century structure called Eastgate House, in High Street, Rochester—once actually a boarding-school for young ladies, and now a Workmen's Institute. On the opposite side of the street is a fine old timbered house, No. 146, which is pointed out as the residence of Sapsea the auctioneer, who is stated to have been drawn from two Rochester personages, one a former mayor and auctioneer, while the wooden effigy "representing Mr. Sapsea's father" (as depicted in the tale) formerly stood over the doorway.

The venerable verger at Rochester Cathedral, Mr. Miles, believes, with some justification, that he is the original of Mr. Tope; the novelist was frequently seen by him to be studying the sacred fane and its precincts most attentively at the time he was engaged upon "Edwin Drood." In another local character, the late veteran Mr. John Brooker, of Higham (whose father planted the famous cedars at Gad's Hill Place), were recognised some of the better qualities and peculiarities of Durdles, although it is suggested that a "drunken old German stonemason" who, some thirty years ago, was always prowling about the Cathedral, was the actual prototype; it seems probable that the effigy of John de Sheppey (A.D. 1360) in the Cathedral gave rise to the conception of Durdles's constant references to the "old uns." Dickens's description of Jasper, the choir-master, is said to have more closely resembled the personality of the organ-bellows blower than that of any other official connected with the Cathedral; his cognomen, however, is still an honoured one in Rochester, the city itself being thinly disguised as "Cloisterham" in the narrative.

"The Mystery of Edwin Drood" was originally intended to comprise twelve monthly parts, but only six of these were published. They were issued by Messrs. Chapman and Hall in the usual green wrappers, demy octavo, at one shilling each, commencing in April, 1870, and ending in September following. Besides a portrait of Dickens engraved on steel, the work contained twelve woodcut illustrations by Luke Fildes, R.A., the same artist being also responsible for the vignette on the title-page of Rochester Cathedral and Castle. Mr. Charles Collins (brother of Mr. Wilkie Collins) was originally thought of as the new illustrator, but this proved impracticable. He designed the cover for the monthly parts, and it is justly considered that here is prefigured the course of the story as intended by Dickens.

In 1870, "Edwin Drood" was published in one volume, cloth, at 7*s.* 6*d.*—*Collation*, pp. viii., 190, with a Prefatory Note, dated "12th August, 1870," referring to the unfinished state in which the story was left at the author's death. It has since been occasionally reissued with or without a date, but is not included in the first Cheap Edition.

The story in parts, as issued, is catalogued at from 6*s.* to 10*s.* The original MS., with memoranda and headings for chapters, is at South Kensington; one folio of the opening of the eleventh chapter, viz., the portion describing Staple Inn, is unfortunately missing.

It may, without exaggeration, be said that no uncompleted work of fiction has excited so much comment, or caused such an amount of conjecture concerning the author's intentions with respect to the plot, as this remarkable fragment of Charles Dickens's last novel, "The Mystery of Edwin Drood."

INDEX.

Elliot Stock, Paternoster Row, London.

www.ingramcontent.com/pod-product-compliance
Lightning Source LLC
Chambersburg PA
CBHW022006050726
47499CB00006BB/1712

* 9 7 8 3 3 3 7 0 2 8 9 2 3 *